In loving memory of Joanna
and our fifty six years together

My grateful thanks to

Beryl, who first encouraged me to write,
all those years ago,
and to Peter, for his friendship and good advice.

Disruptive daylight
Illuminating dark corners,
Searchlighting reality.

Dreams, memories, fantasies
Wait patiently for darkness.
Just close your eyes, concentrate –

The unreal world vanishes

hors de combat /ˌor de ˈkōbaː/ *adj.* out of the fight, disabled. (F)

one

He started to sweat and the sudden pain in his chest took his breath away. His ears were buzzing and he felt himself falling. The pain stabbed deeper and, from a long way away, he heard a voice calling, shouting to him.

The bright light hurt his eyes. Someone was bending over him, speaking softly.
 "Your age? How old are you?"
He tried hard to remember, but the effort was too great.
 "Religion?"
He narrowed his eyes against the bright light and tried to concentrate.

The question brought back a flood of memories – thirty years earlier, in the war, before he met Joanna. It must have been 1940, during the Blitz. He remembered lying on a makeshift stretcher, wrapped in blankets against the cold, looking up at the great domed ceiling of the Middlesex Hospital entrance hall, watching the cracks widen with each explosion and waiting for the whole lot to come crashing down. And now here she was, the same recording angel, the same fatuous question.

 "I can't quite hear you – shall I put down 'Church of England'?"

He couldn't make up his mind then and he couldn't make up his mind now. Perhaps he should settle for C of E to be on the safe side. Pity one couldn't carry a card, donating one's soul to the appropriate authority when the time came.

The recording angel continued in her soft, gentle voice. "Next of kin?"

So he was going to die, was he? Perhaps it was time he stopped messing around and made up his mind, one way or the other, before it was too late.

Gentle hands lifted him and someone drew a curtain, cutting out the bright light. He opened his eyes and a beautiful creature with long, dark hair was standing over him. Surely he wasn't in Paradise already? On second thoughts, unlikely – angels, as far as he could remember, had blonde hair. This angel, blonde hair or not, was so beautiful that he wanted to reach out and hold her, but she stuck something into his arm and went away.

There was a strange rustling noise and they were lying on a couch in a villa with a white marble balcony. The windows were open and the white silken curtains rustled gently in the soft evening breeze as they kissed for the first time. There was a bright white moon in a deep blue sky and they were very much in love.

'On such a night as this, when the sweet wind did gently kiss the trees and they did make no noise.'

"The damned woman's done it again!"

Opening his eyes, Francis and saw a tall, thin man crouched over him.

"How can I be expected to do my job properly after *she's* been messing around?"

How indeed.

"I'm dreadfully sorry," said Francis. Best to be on the safe side.

"Not your fault," said the tall, thin man. "It's that damned Indian doctor, she keeps taking my vein."

So that's who she was, the beautiful creature with the long dark hair. Perhaps she wanted the vein to weave herself a sari to wear at his funeral. If so, then he could die peacefully in the knowledge that she would be there.

He dozed off, willing himself to return to the villa with the white marble balcony and the white silken curtains rustling in the breeze – and there she was, lying beside him. The blue shadows wove a pattern of blue and silver around her breasts as she turned towards him. She kissed him again – beautifully, smoothly, frantically. She lay on top of him and wrapped her golden legs around him. Her desire overwhelmed him and her long nails dug deep into his arm.

The pain jolted him awake. God, how his arm hurt. He looked up and saw a dark red bag, with a tube leading to his left arm. He was trying to work that one out when he saw the tall, thin man, still hovering, like a broody hen deprived of its egg.

"You do realise of course that this transfusion should have been in your right arm – I'm your anaesthetist and your left arm belongs to me – she had no right to take it – it makes my job so much more difficult."

If only the wretched fellow would go away so that he could get back to his villa, to his beautiful Indian doctor. He shouldn't have left her like that. What a silly thing to do.

Francis turned on his side, trying to recapture the magic moment, but it was too late.

Early childhood memories intervened, clamouring for attention – memories that he'd done his best to forget.

Gentle Jesus, meek and mild, look upon a little child, pity my simplicity, suffer me to come to thee, Amen.

Night after night after bloody night, sweet and sickly, suffocating, paralysing. Year after year of smothering until he felt he'd burst if it went on much longer. His mother had always wanted a girl, so he never really had a chance. She would tiptoe into his room every night, every bloody night, and they would sing *Gentle Jesus* together, right the way through. Then if the rendering had been less than perfect, if there had been a single mistake – right the way through again, several times if need be. He would clench his fists and will himself to hang on until the final *Amen*, then he knew that the ordeal was over – that he'd be safe until tomorrow.

All he had to do then was to close his eyes and pretend to be asleep, anything to be rid of her. She would bend down and embrace him and he would hold his breath until she had tiptoed out of the room, then all his rage and frustration would pour out in one huge, gasping sigh. He would scream and scream – ever so quietly – until the sickly sweet, cloying, suffocating feeling had gone. Then he would get out of bed, open the window, take several deep breaths of fresh air until he stopped shaking, climb back into bed and listen to Henry Hall on his wireless until he fell asleep.

The only time he felt free was when he was down in the basement. He would ride round and round on his tricycle – hundreds, thousands of times – making as much noise as he could, so that – if she called for him – he could always pretend he hadn't heard her. The steps leading down to the basement were quite steep and he knew she'd never bother to come all the way down, so he was safe enough until it was time for tea, when he would have to sit quietly in a chair and not make a noise until it was time to escape again.

His most cherished possession was an old gramophone in a wooden cabinet. The cabinet had flaps on three sides, which could be opened or shut to increase or decrease the volume of the record. Francis had soon discovered that the combination of a loud needle and fully opened flaps was all that was necessary to bring on one of his mother's headaches, thus ensuring that the gramophone would, sooner or later, be consigned to the basement. And so it was, sooner rather than later, that the magnificent instrument became his very own, together with a pile of wonderful twelve-inch Aeolian records with black and gold labels.

He couldn't quite read the labels, so he played them all, one by one, and soon got to know the ones he liked best. These he could identify by the varying patterns made by the labels as they spun round and round on the gramophone. It never occurred to him to mark them in any way – he just knew which was which – and, the more he played them, the more one record in particular stood out head and shoulders above the rest.

He copied out the labels, laboriously, on a piece of paper. At first sight, each side of the record seemed the same, with the word 'Overture' in large black lettering, but there the similarity ended. He could just decipher the faint lettering. One side was Rossini's *William Tell* and the other side was Tchaikovsky's *1812*. He asked his mother what *1812* signified and she told him it was a famous battle when the Russians defeated Napoleon. He didn't know who Napoleon was, but the 'famous battle' was great fun, particularly if he opened all the flaps on the gramophone and used an extra loud needle. The tricycle was his trusty steed as he raced round and round the basement. Bells clanged and canons roared as the enemy scattered and fled before the onslaught.

"Don't play the gramophone any more to-day, dear. I think I've a headache coming." His mother stood on the basement steps with her hand on her forehead and the enemy escaped to fight another day.

His mother was always having headaches. They followed her around like gigantic spiders and, if she accidentally left one behind, there would always be another one in the next room, lurking in wait, ready to pounce. As soon as she entered the room, particularly if someone was speaking or making a noise, she would clap her hand to her forehead and the spider would be there. The headache could sometimes be postponed if the room was empty or they were sitting quietly, but the trouble with a postponed headache was that it was far more disruptive than an instant headache. Not only was it more intense, but it invariably lasted longer and could therefore be relied upon to ruin the entire day. It had, so to speak, improved with age and, if postponed for long enough, it was guaranteed to ruin the evening. It had even been known to last through the night and well into the next day.

A headache was obviously on its way, so Francis decided that, on balance, it was better for all concerned to get it over and done with as soon as possible. He increased the speed of the gramophone until the gold lettering in the middle of the record streaked into a blur. Needles didn't last long at that speed, but the noise of battle became a deafening screech and his mother retreated rapidly with her hands over her ears. With any luck, her headache would be over and done with in no time.

"Ah, there you are, dear, I think I'm feeling better already. Come and sit down and have a nice cup of tea."

The next day was Sunday – the day that Aunty Phoebe came to lunch. Aunty Phoebe was a large, bony woman with big red hands and a blue nose. Her hands were always cold, even in summer, and she had a deep, gruff voice. Somehow she reminded Francis of a witch, but she was kind and generous and he was very fond of her. She was his father's sister and Francis always knew when she was coming, because the bottles of beer on the sideboard were hidden away before she came. He never knew why, but he had overheard her saying something about the demon drink, so perhaps she didn't like beer very much.

"I'm afraid I'm not very well to-day, Phoebe. I've a dreadful headache."

His mother was standing in the hallway, looking pale and distraught. She was supporting herself against the wall with one hand while the other clutched her forehead.

Francis suddenly felt guilty – perhaps he'd overdone it yesterday after all. He must have speeded up the record so much that she couldn't get up the steps in time, thus triggering off not only an instant headache, but a postponed headache as well. How awful. He'd have to be more careful in future.

His father came downstairs looking pale, mother's headache must have lasted all night. Father was always at home on Sundays and Francis looked forward to lunch.

"Where's Phoebe?" he asked.

"Oh, she's gone home – I told her I had a bad headache."

"Good, I'll be able to have my beer now – I really miss it on Sundays."

Francis couldn't understand why father missed his beer on Sundays when it was all there, hidden away in the sideboard – he must have known it was there – and what it had to do with Aunty Phoebe, goodness only knew. There was so much he didn't know that he'd almost given up trying to understand. He wasn't even allowed to play with the other boys in the road. His mother said they were 'common' and he didn't know what that meant at first until she explained to him the difference between being middle class and working class. It didn't make sense to him and, for the first time in his life, he openly defied her. He knew it would bring on one of her headaches, but he didn't mind. She'd brought it upon herself.

He went out to the gate to talk to his friends – at least, he did so hope they would be his friends – but his mother intervened.

"Francis – come back here, dear – fancy going out without your coat – you'll catch your death of cold."

Everything blurred after that – his first act of open defiance.

"I hate you," he shouted "I hate you, I hate you, I hate you, I hate you. . ."

"For goodness sake, be quiet, or you'll wake everyone up."

Someone was bending over him, shaking him gently, speaking in a low, gentle voice.

"People often have bad dreams when they're in hospital," she said.

"This wasn't a bad dream, nurse – I was remembering things that happened when I was young – things I'd almost forgotten."

She smiled. "We all try to suppress unhappy memories," she said. "It never works in the long run – they always return, sooner or later. Now, stop shaking and try to settle down – and mind that drip, you'll pull it out if you're not careful."

He looked up at her, gratefully.

"That's better," she said. "I'm glad it's not me you hate."

Bright lights, noise and bustle – busy day ahead. An army of cleaners were at work, soldier ants, picking everything clean. They surged forward, remorselessly.

"Guess who she went out with last night?"

King Kong? – or perhaps the Loch Ness Monster.

"Anyway, she told 'im to keep 'is bloody 'ands to 'imself. Then she got out o' the car and walked 'ome. Raining it was, too."

"Serve 'er right, that's what I say."

The electric polishers clattered away and the beds shunted to and fro.

"Sorry, dearie – only a drop o' water – soon mop it up."

Their cheerful, uncomplicated chatter was infectious and Francis tried to join in.

"What's that, dearie? Sorry, can't hear a word you say."

The beds crashed back against the walls and the hurricane blew itself out.

Nurses emerged from hiding and began to clear up the mess. They mopped up more water, rescued the flowers and re-made the beds, just in time for Matron's round.

"Nurse – what's wrong with this man's arm? See to it right away."

Curtains drawn – his favourite nurse, fortunately.

"Now then – let's see what you've been doing to yourself."

Francis tensed, waiting for the fresh incision, trying to appear nonchalant.

"There now – that didn't hurt, did it?"

She leaned over to take his blood pressure and he couldn't resist a little cuddle.

She seemed not to notice and he'd just decided to have another go when further exploration was interrupted by the arrival of a small, pompous looking man with a military moustache.

"Can I have him now, nurse?"

"You certainly can – and you're welcome to him, too."

The man smiled – a tight lipped smile – and placed a large black case at the foot of his bed.

"ECG," he announced, crisply. "Jacket off – come on – I don't have all day

Obviously a man of few words. Pity he couldn't say 'please'. Come to think of it, hardly anyone in the hospital ever said 'please'.

Francis took off his pyjama jacket and the man produced some red and black wires with terminals on one end and suction pads on the other. The suction pads were clamped to his chest and Francis winced in pain. The man was obviously a bomb disposal expert on secondment to the hospital to deal with unstable patients.

"Take a deep breath, then relax and breathe gently until I tell you to stop."

Just as he thought. Deep breath, then five, four, three, two, one, zero.

UNEXPLODED PATIENT DEFUSED
BOMB EXPERT AWARDED OBE.

"Breathe normally now and lie still while I remove the pads."

The bomb disposal man ripped off the pads and Francis winced again. The man smiled, the same, tight lipped smile. He was clearly a sadist and Francis wondered if he ought to apologise for not exploding, but thought better of it.

"Don't just lie there, man – put your jacket on – I haven't got all day you know."

"Thank you very much," said Francis, politely.

The man snorted, picked up his case and departed without a backward glance. Maybe he was not used to being thanked, however sarcastically. He reminded Francis of someone he knew, someone particularly horrible. Who was it now?

two

Of course, Major Peel. His first headmaster. He closed his eyes and tried to concentrate on Major Peel. As if he'd ever forget his first day at Hazelhurst.

> Parents assembling in the hall, the overpowering heat, Major Peel exuding charm, Mrs Peel carrying all before, doting mothers with their reluctant offspring, a sense of foreboding. Francis didn't really know why, he only knew he didn't like Major Peel.
> They all filed into his study, out through the French windows and into the garden.
> Major Peel was known for his sweet peas, which he cultivated in a huge greenhouse adjoining the study. They followed him into the greenhouse while he enthused about the varieties he had managed to grow.
> "What a charming man – and such a delightful wife, too."
> They had no way of knowing what lay in store for their precious offspring, but the sweet peas and the cream cakes which lay in store for them had done their job. Hazelhurst was obviously an excellent choice.
> The last parent had scarcely departed before Major Peel's charm underwent a dramatic change. He strode out into the greenhouse and returned with a thin bamboo cane, which he waved in the air with a swishing noise before slamming it down on the table, narrowly missing the last of the cream cakes.
> The boys huddled together in terror as he shouted out the rules, each rule preceded by a deafening crash. There were so many rules that the tablecloth was soon festooned with an intricate criss-cross pattern, which

wove its way skillfully between the cups and saucers. The penalties for non-compliance with any rule were even more deafening, with several strokes in quick succession emphasizing the extent of the punishment. The boys gazed helplessly at the last cream cake, which had somehow avoided being squashed, but which finally leaped into the air and landed upside down in a crumpled heap on the floor. A sad, forgotten remnant of their childhood.

"Shall I clear the table now, dear?"

Mrs Peel, relieved no doubt that her best china had survived the commencement of yet another term, seemed remarkably unconcerned and Major Peel's bloodshot eyes began to lose their fervour. He sat down, breathing heavily, and his smile returned – a thin, tight lipped smile.

"Certainly, dear. I was just making sure that the new boys understood the rules."

They soon discovered that the rules were never the same for very long. They varied from day to day according to the exigencies of the moment, with the result that no one was ever able to remember the new rules sufficiently well to avoid punishment.

One such exigency was the Dell, a wooded copse adjoining the cricket field. Ownership of the Dell had been in dispute for some while. It quite obviously belonged to a neighbouring farmer, but Major Peel had been in the habit of collecting firewood there ever since he arrived and, over the years, had persuaded himself that it was part of the school. The very thought of surrender was anathema to him. What he had, he held.

Soon the school flag flew defiantly from the topmost tree and solicitors pondered the niceties of trespass. When the first writ arrived, Major Peel summoned the entire school and read it out aloud, his voice trembling with emotion. They had never heard of a writ before and some of the younger boys thought it was a passage from the Old Testament. He held it aloft and pledged the school to defend its heritage from thieving farmers, then he tore it into shreds and threw the pieces in the air. The call to arms was rapturously received and there was a wild scramble for the pieces, which soon became collectors' items, bartered for sweets and marbles. The next writ arrived a week later and was ceremoniously burned, while the Dell became a hive of activity. The chopping of firewood intensified and the entire school gathered there each day for tracking and nature studies. The farmer seemed to have lost interest and Major Peel even went so far as to congratulate the whole school at assembly. Their victory was short lived.

The farmer was in no particular hurry. He lived by the seven year rotation of crops and knew the value of patience. He bided his time, secure in the knowledge that he had the law on his side, a few more weeks wouldn't make any difference in the long run. He waited until the firewood had piled up and then he struck. Swiftly, silently and effectively. The boys woke up one morning to find the Dell fenced off with a double row of stakes and barbed wire. Major Peel was incoherent with rage, but there was nothing he could do about it, he'd been out-manoeuvred and the farmer had the law on his side. Foraging parties crept through the wire at dead of night to rescue the firewood, but they were too late. The farmer had taken the lot. Overcome with grief at his loss, Major Peel instantly changed the rules. He accused the foraging parties of trespass and, with aching bottoms, they shared with him the humiliation of his defeat.

The boys had no way of knowing it, but this particular set back was the least of Major Peel's problems. The school was on the verge of bankruptcy and each post brought its fair share of bills and final demands. He would see the postman coming up the drive and would wait just inside the porch until the brown envelopes cascaded through the letter box, then he would leap out, confronting the postman and threatening to set the dog on him. A particularly large bill would drive him to the verge of hysteria and a final demand would be shredded in mid air, decimated with his bamboo cane as it floated to the ground. He had an uncanny instinct for final demands and the slashed, unopened envelopes bore mute testimony to the accuracy of his aim.

He was an individualist if nothing else and any connection between the school fees and the actual cost of boarding and tuition had long been coincidental. Parents were charged at random according to their supposed ability to pay and there were staggering variations in the fees, with some parents paying anything up to twice as much as others. Bills were submitted haphazardly and the same parents sometimes received several bills for varying amounts. Parents in the know would wait for a comparatively small bill to arrive and would then pay it immediately, whereupon Major Peel, delighted to receive a cheque of any sort, would assume that the correct amount had been paid.

It was a long, hard winter. The loss of the firewood had been more serious than imagined and the coal bills mounted. The History master and the English master left and only Matron and Jenkins, the gardener, remained. Major Peel himself taught Maths and Jenkins taught History and English.

The trolley reeked of stale vegetables and the smell was revolting. Hazelhurst faded abruptly as Francis did his best not to be sick. He had an absolute horror of institutions and the dinner trolley, its contents already congealing, was an integral part of that horror. To-day's offering was cottage pie followed by semolina pudding. His stomach heaved again and he lay back, gasping.

"Now what's wrong?"

"I wonder if I could have some fish?

"Fish? – where d'you think you are, at the Ritz?"

All was well – he could tell from the sound of her voice that fish was on the way. Steamed fish and mashed potato were always there, somewhere, but it needed patience to coax them out. The daily ritual of pretending there was no fish was so well established that he needed all his cunning to ensure that it came his way. The other patients, their mouths full of cottage pie, glared at him, but no matter – in a survival situation it was every man for himself. He chewed the tasteless fish, contentedly.

three

Francis dozed off after lunch – all he had to do was to concentrate and he could remember anything he wanted.

He drifted on, half asleep half awake, as memories crowded in, jostling for recognition. Perhaps – if he concentrated, he could select them at random, but Hazelhurst kept intruding, demanding his attention.

> Major Peel's devotion to the noble art of boxing was such that it often overshadowed the entire curriculum – probably just as well, considering the shortage of teachers. He organised it like a military campaign, every boy in the school having to fight every other boy until blood was drawn. A surprising number of boys reported sick on boxing days and the new matron had her hands full, although it should be said that this sudden onslaught of injury was not entirely due to boxing, but to something far more interesting – Matron's knickers.
>
> The sick bay consisted of three mattresses, side by side at the end of the landing, with a curtain to keep out the germs. There should have been three beds as well, but Major Peel's attitude towards illness was unequivocal. Illness, like prison, should be made as uncomfortable as possible, thus ensuring a speedy recovery. He had therefore removed the beds and, had he had his own way, the mattresses would have gone as well, but the new matron had intervened and, disarmed by her freckles, he had relented.

They were all in love with Matron. She was young, she was pretty and, above all, she wore the most delightful knickers. The removal of the beds from the sick bay made their discovery almost inevitable, the mattresses on the floor enabling their occupants to see a great deal more than intended – and so it was with Matron.

Boys too ill to raise their heads would whisper something and she would bend down to minister to them, each act of mercy enabling the occupant of the next mattress to have a good look. Then, as he in turn moaned and groaned, his neighbour was afforded an equally delightful view. There was strong competition for the mattress in the middle, from whence could be procured, as it were, a double vision of delight.

It was generally agreed that the colours varied from day to day and six different colours were positively identified, a different colour for each day of the week. The sick bay was closed on Sundays so they had no easy way of finding out about the seventh colour, and although they hung around after church in the hope of a gust of wind, they never did find out. Majority opinion favoured virginal white.

In the meantime, boxing reigned supreme. Whenever it rained, or looked as though it might rain, the ring would be prepared under Major Peel's supervision. Woodworm had played havoc with the floor of the gym and the corner posts sagged alarmingly. This caused him considerable concern.

"Just think what would happen," he would say, "if one of the posts collapsed. A boy might be injured." Impressed by this sudden concern for their welfare, the reluctant heroes would heave the posts into place, wriggling them from side to side in the vain hope that one of them actually would collapse, trying desperately to postpone the inevitable. A sharp swish of the cane would send them cowering, trying not to catch his eye. This was the moment he really enjoyed. He would line them up in a row and stalk up and down behind them, swishing his cane in the air. The first two boys to flinch would be grabbed from behind and rushed into the ring for slaughter.

"Three rounds Queensberry rules," he would shout, and battle would commence. They had no idea what the Queensberry rules were, so they closed their eyes, flailed their fists and hoped for the best. They soon discovered that hitting below the belt meant instant disqualification, so fouls were numerous and belts were worn higher and higher.

Major Peel would clutch his cane in one hand and a large white towel in the other and wait for the magic moment when blood was drawn, whereupon he would throw in the towel, which would skim over the ropes and envelop the hapless loser. The towel soon became saturated, making it difficult to decide whether fresh blood had been drawn or whether it had actually come from a previous victim, whereupon Major Peel, seemingly satisfied, cried a halt to the carnage and threw the towel to Sally, his mongrel terrier, whom he kept for the express purpose of killing the rats living under the gym.

Major Peel faded. Just as well really, considering what a sadist he was, and hospital life intervened.

"Why didn't you come to physiotherapy this morning?"

Why indeed? Francis considered various possible excuses and decided that the truth was probably the most effective.

"I'm afraid I forgot, Sister. Doctor Newman said it wasn't all that important until after my operation."

Problem solved for the time being. Francis decided that he would have a second go at remembering another moment when time stood still. If he concentrated sufficiently, he might be able to blot out Major Peel and all he stood for. He closed his eyes, but the magic wouldn't come.

"Still mumbling to yourself? You haven't been drinking, have you?"

Chance would be a fine thing.

"What time is it, nurse?"

"Three o'clock in the morning – you've been asleep since lunchtime and now you wake everyone up in the middle of the night."

"My back's aching, nurse – just there."

Her cool hands explored the small of his back and he shivered in anticipation.

"Not there – a bit further down."

"Get on with you – you're a proper old fraud."

Francis smiled to himself and settled down as best he could for the rest of the night. Tomorrow he would be cut open, one more day before the sacrifice, and then what? He preferred not to think about it. Even Hazelhurst would be better than the shiver of fear which was beginning to haunt his memories and his dreams. Better to stay awake now and concentrate on the memories which were beginning to take over his life, or what was left of it, memories which, for him, were much more real than the unreal world of the hospital ward.

> Apart from boxing and caning, Major Peel's great love was the Stage. Anything that took place on a stage was meat and drink to him and the rickety old platform in the gym at Hazelhurst was the scene of many musical and cultural events. The highlight of the year was the Hazelhurst Choral Society's annual concert, rehearsals for which commenced at the beginning of the Christmas term and conveniently ensured that no lessons needed to be given. The rehearsals for the

concert involved almost continuous shouting and cursing at all those boys rash enough to participate, but they didn't mind. It was better than lessons and, as their singing improved, they almost started to enjoy what they were doing. Jenkins played the piano, an old, upright piano, with a tendency to emit loud, twanging noises from time to time, but quite at random, so that they never knew exactly when the twang would come. They would wait for it and nothing happened, then, quite suddenly, several twangs in quick succession would reduce them all to helpless laughter. Jenkins, who was in charge of rehearsals when Major Peel was absent, would play on, apparently unaware of the twangs and their effect on the chorus. All in all, the boys thoroughly enjoyed the rehearsals – no lessons, no boxing, very little beating and something to look forward to for a change.

The Christmas concert was invariably the cultural event of the year. Parents came from far and wide, and they were seldom disappointed. Major Peel – "such a charming man" – always conducted the concerts himself, shouting at the boys who were out of tune, but smiling at the same time so that the parents wouldn't know he was in a rage.

One memorable production was *The Pied Piper of Hamelin*, which events transpired to stamp with the seal of greatness. The stage, suitably decorated, had a concealed hosepipe to provide water for the river Weser. Major Peel was nothing if not thorough and the dress rehearsal was a great success, with water flowing across the stage and disappearing through the cracks in the floor, thus lending authenticity to the event. The water pressure would be increased during the finale to lend dramatic emphasis to the production.

News of the innovation soon spread. The gym was packed for the occasion, with standing room only at the back, and the capacity audience applauded wildly as the river flowed. The water level rose and the rats under the floorboard started to squeak, quietly at first and then with increasing volume as their habitat was flooded. The sudden appearance of a real, live rat sparked off more frantic applause and the rat, greatly alarmed, scampered across the river Weser and disappeared backstage. Its sudden reappearance in time for the curtain call brought the house down and the cheering and clapping lasted a good five minutes. Major Peel, greatly encouraged, announced even more ambitious plans for the coming year, but it was not to be.

It had been rumoured for some time that the ship was sinking. In a last, desperate attempt to keep it afloat, he announced that girls would be admitted at reduced fees. To forestall any possible criticism, he wrote to all parents, explaining that girls were cheaper to keep than boys – they ate less and they did not need expensive boxing lessons. They certainly had a civilising influence. Beating and rat catching diminished and the boys were initiated into the perils of mixed hockey. The girls invariably won with a mixture of fouls and histrionics which had to be seen and heard to be believed. But the new venture was short lived. The sole remaining teacher left when his salary cheque bounced for the third time and Matron departed shortly after, probably for the same reason. Only Jenkins remained. He had nowhere else to go.

With his usual resourcefulness, Major Peel divided the remaining pupils into seniors and juniors. He taught the seniors himself and Jenkins taught the juniors, but the curriculum inevitably suffered. Any connection between the curriculum and what was actually taught had long been tenuous and it now became more of a farce than ever. First to go was Latin, followed by Physics and Chemistry. They had never actually done any Physics or Chemistry, but it had always been there, on the timetable, and it was now officially deleted.

The classrooms were icy cold and the most popular subjects were those that lent themselves to role play. Jenkins had never taught History before, but he took to it like a duck to water. The Boer War was one of his favourites, with the relief of Mafeking providing a splendid opportunity of keeping warm. The history class took over the abandoned classroom next door and they took it in turns to be the spirited defenders and the Boers, while Jenkins led the relief column. It was much better than boxing. Encouraged by his success, Jenkins embarked on Theology with equal enthusiasm, the Old Testament providing ample opportunity for warlike encounters. Even Geography was eventually narrowed down to a series of landings by Christopher Columbus in the teeth of ferocious opposition. The two classrooms soon became permanent battlegrounds and, as one battle succeeded another, the boys were often hard put to remember which subject was actually being taught. The lessons were a huge success and even Major Peel was impressed.

four

The sound of battle waned as visiting time brought a flurry of activity. Chairs were removed and stacked neatly in the corners so that visitors could collect them and bring them back again. The patients were propped up in bed and tucked in so tightly that they could hardly move. Then the floodgates opened and an avalanche of visitors cascaded into the ward and settled gradually between the beds. Francis, who had no visitors, pretended to be asleep.

"Hi, Pop."

Good God – Richard – and, behind him, Joanna, her bright eyes strained and tired. So they'd come after all, all that way, just to see him before he went to the slaughter. Joanna hugged him and smiled, the same shy smile, though the tears weren't far away. Francis stopped feeling sorry for himself and, long after they'd gone, the strength of their coming stayed with him, giving him the courage to face whatever lay ahead.

> It was nineteen forty-one and they were both nineteen. Francis was so much in love that he simply had to tell her. It was now or never. The river bank sparkled in the moonlight and they stood on the bridge, hand in hand, watching while the silver river flowed quietly towards the sea. It was the perfect moment, but he still hesitated. He hadn't yet told her what the problem was. He'd already lost most of his friends and he couldn't bear the thought of losing her as well. A

conscientious objector in wartime can hardly expect to be popular.

They lived in the same small town, but they'd only met a few weeks ago and it was unlikely that she already knew, although it was only a matter of time. She had told him about her two brothers in the army and her elder sister's boyfriend in the navy, so the knowledge that he was a conchie was bound to come as a shock and he just didn't know how she would react. Each day that passed made it more and more difficult for him to explain why he hadn't told her before, always assuming of course that she'd bother to listen. Serve him right – a conchie, but without the guts to tell her.

"Joanna. . ." he began, but she wasn't listening.

"What's that?" she asked. She was looking across the river at a line of sacks, hanging on a frame and clearly visible in the bright moonlight. What indeed!

"Those," he said, "are old sacks stuffed with straw – they use them for bayonet practice."

She looked at him, perhaps not realising the enormity of it all, and his frustrations suddenly exploded.

"Obscene!" he shouted. "Isn't it obscene?"

She drew back, startled.

"I'm sorry," he said. "I didn't mean to frighten you, but there's only one word to describe it."

"Tell me about it." Her voice was quiet and she squeezed his arm as if to reassure him.

"They come here every week and learn how to kill people. You have to pretend that the sack is your enemy. You stick your bayonet into his stomach, then you twist it so that the bayonet rips him open when you pull it out. The idea is that regular bayonet practice hardens you and makes killing automatic – bayonet in, twist, pull – bayonet in, twist, pull. Isn't that revolting?"

She turned away and he was suddenly full of remorse. He needn't have been so explicit.

He put his arm around her and saw that she was crying. His whole future hung in the balance, then she looked up at him and smiled and he knew that he wouldn't have to explain anything. She was on his side now and always would be. The Ministry of Labour however, had other ideas.

Francis had been expecting some sort of Court Room – prisoner in the dock and Magistrates sitting on high – but this room was surprisingly ordinary, quite bare except for a few tables and chairs. The sort of room used for dealing with dissidents, although he had to admit that his own interrogation had been remarkably fair – so far. Perhaps the worst was still to come.

He studied the three men facing him while he waited for the next question. The large man in the centre was obviously the Chairman of the Tribunal. He was the one asking the questions – routine questions about his background and beliefs. Francis had done his best to reply honestly: no, he didn't attend any church; no, he hadn't discussed his pacifism with his parents; no, he hadn't thought about it seriously before the War – except, perhaps, when he had refused to join the Officer Training Corps at his boarding school.

The Chairman had paused and was writing something on a scrap of paper, presumably for the benefit of his colleagues. "Why did you refuse?" he asked.

"I don't know really – it was supposed to be voluntary and I just didn't want to."

"What was the reaction?"

"There was quite a row about it."

"I'm not surprised. Now answer me this – you've already told us that you don't attend church – would you call yourself a Christian?"

"No, not really, I suppose I'm an Atheist."

The Chairman made another note and Francis realised that he'd made a tactical error. He almost knew what would come next.

"So, you don't go to church and you've just told us that you are an Atheist, that you don't believe in God. How can an Atheist have a conscientious objection?"

How indeed? A pivotal question and it needed a sensible answer. Francis tried to collect his thoughts.

"You do know of course that there are plenty of good jobs in the Army that don't involve killing?"

The man in uniform seated next to the Chairman glared at Francis with ill-disguised hostility and Francis glared back as he continued with his interruption.

"The Pioneer Corps for instance, or, if you don't fancy that, we now have the Non-Combatant Corps specially for people like you who don't like the idea of fighting for their country, but are prepared to serve in other ways."

Trust him to play the patriotic card, and a sneaky one too. A seemingly attractive alternative, but, if you thought about it, all that did was to salve your own precious conscience at the expense of some other poor bugger, who would then be sent out to kill or be killed – it just wasn't good enough.

"I'm not prepared to do that," said Francis, firmly.

The Chairman looked up, frowning.

"You haven't answered my question yet – how can you say that you have a conscientious objection if you don't believe in God?"

Francis was almost grateful for the interruption. It had given him time to think.

"I just feel that it is morally wrong for young men to be sent out to kill each other."

"Very well. We've spent quite enough time on this case. We will adjourn for five minutes while we consider what to do with you."

They filed out and Francis relaxed. The sheer absurdity of trying to convince them of his sincerity in such a short time gave the whole thing an air of unreality, but he'd done his best and the rest was in the lap of the gods. He smiled to himself at the thought – an apt phrase for an unreal situation.

The questioning reminded him of his previous brush with authority, at his public school, before the War. . .

"You do realise that I shall have to inform your parents that you have refused to join the Officer

Training Corps – I don't know what's come over you – don't you want to defend your country?"

"Against whom, sir?"

"*Whom* do you *think*? The Bolsheviks of course."

"How about the Germans, sir?"

"Don't be impudent – the Germans too, of course – anyone who threatens the British Empire. All boys join the Corps at sixteen unless they have a medical certificate."

"I thought it was voluntary, sir."

"Of course it's voluntary – we have a fine tradition of voluntary service in this country – that's why I find your refusal so disgraceful. You're a disgrace to your school, a disgrace to your parents and a disgrace to your country."

"Yes, sir."

"Is that all you have to say? Very well – I shall report you to the Headmaster and he will decide what to do with you."

It often seemed to Francis that people in authority spent far too much time trying to decide what to do with him. Now this lot were doing the same, but at least they'd given him the opportunity of explaining how he felt before sentencing.

Here they came now, taking their seats, shuffling their papers. The moment of truth had arrived.

"Stand up, please."

Francis stood and faced them. He felt surprisingly calm.

"We have decided to allow you conditional exemption – that is exemption from military service provided that you undertake certain work under civilian control for the duration of the War. You will work either in agriculture, forestry, land drainage or in a hospital and you have one month in which to comply with this condition. My colleague here from the Ministry of Labour will ensure that you comply and he will assist you in finding suitable work if necessary."

So that's who he was, the third man, the one who hadn't spoken was now responsible for him. Thank goodness it wasn't the Army Captain.

"Thank you, sir." And that was that, just what he'd hoped for. Francis now knew exactly what he wanted to do. He'd never worked in a hospital before, but helping to save life instead of destroying it made everything worth while. Joanna would come with him and they'd start a new life together.

five

Francis awoke, strangely elated, concentrating on the battle to come. He tried to stop shaking, but the thought of being cut open wasn't very pleasant and his courage gradually evaporated as he waited for the slaughter. Perhaps a prayer or two might help him relax. He was still wondering when he felt a prick in his arm. Probably too late now, anyway. The trolley arrived and gathered speed. It crashed through the swing doors and raced along the passage.

"Charge," he shouted, and his courage returned. The 1812 overture rang in his ears and the trolley hurtled forward at breakneck speed, mowing down the enemy. A dagger pierced his arm and everything suddenly stopped. The angels in white were waiting for him and one of them told him to count up to ten, then the angels blurred and pain tore at him like a tiger. He surfaced, screaming, and football faces swam in and out of focus.

"Not too bad, considering – better leave him for a while and see what happens."

He tried to focus, but the football faces turned into red and blue masks, red for pain, blue for death. The red masks were winning now. They merged into a huge red shroud, flying towards him, enveloping him, suffocating him.

> Francis was looking up at a huge four-storey building with stone steps leading up to an impressive front

entrance, all archways and marble pillars. Probably a stately home at the turn of the century and now being put to better use. The notice in front stated: 'District Hospital – Main Entrance – No Parking'.

He pushed open the rusty iron gate at the side of the entrance and looked around. The usual collection of cars and ambulances and a small wooden hut with a half-opened door. There was a hand-written notice above the door, 'Porter's Lodge – Visitors report here.' Typical, he thought, opulence in front, but cheese-paring behind, where all the work was done. He pushed open the door and looked inside.

"Come in. At least you're on time, which is more than can be said for some of your lot." Francis wondered vaguely what he meant, but he did glance at the clock, just to make sure. 8 a.m. on the dot, thank goodness.

"Come in and close the door behind you – and sit down, too – I don't like people standing up and peering down at me while I speak to them. I've got a stiff neck. That's what comes of sitting in a draught all day. Now – what's your name?"

Francis handed over his identity card and the man checked his name against a list on the table in front of him. Then, without speaking to Francis, he opened a hatch in the wall beside him.

"Number fourteen just arrived – what shall I do with him?"

So people were still discussing what to do with him. And why a number instead of a name? Perhaps he'd come to a lunatic asylum by mistake.

"Better put him on Casualty for the time being – we'll sort him out later."

The voice of cold command slammed the hatch and Francis felt an instant dislike for whoever was inside. How strange to dislike someone you haven't even seen.

"Don't worry about him – he always puts people off to start with, but he's OK really. I'm the Head Porter, by the way – I'm the one responsible for you lot."

"I hope you don't mind my asking," said Francis, "but I don't think I know anyone else here. What do you mean by 'you lot'?"

38

"You'll find out soon enough. All I'm interested in is that you arrive on time, leave on time, and keep your nose clean. I suppose you'll be wanting a cup of tea? Come on then, I'll show you the porter's rest room."

He stood up and buttoned his uniform, then he led the way around the side of the main building to a much larger hut. He threw open the door and looked inside. "Wakey-wakey – here's another one for you." And, to Francis, "Wait here until I come to fetch you."

There were two men sitting at the table, drinking tea. Both quite young, about his own age. "I'm Giles," said the younger of the two – a slim, dark haired man with an expressive face. "Welcome to the madhouse – yes, that's right, another bloody conchie. Have a cup of tea."

"How did you know?" asked Francis.

"Just guessed – takes one to know one. That's Ray, by the way – he's one of us, too."

Ray went on reading the paper. Francis sat down opposite him but he didn't look up. He was unkempt and unshaven, with black greasy hair and dirty grey overalls. He seemed to sense that Francis was looking at him, as he got up almost immediately, said something to Francis in a strong northcountry accent, threw down his paper and left. Obviously a man of few words.

"Don't mind him," said Giles, plonking down a mug of tea. "He's the stuff of which martyrs are made – d'you know, he actually volunteered to do the bins, the filthiest job of all – the job we'd all been avoiding."

"Why was that?" asked Francis.

"Can't you guess? – everything goes in the bins – surgical waste, bloodstained swabs, cancerous lungs, bits of arms and legs from the Theatre, gangrenous residue – Ray collects it all and dumps it in the incinerator room. How would you like a job like that, all day and every day?"

No wonder he was unkempt and unshaven. Francis felt quite ashamed of himself. Fancy passing judgement on someone who had actually volunteered to do the worst job in the hospital.

Giles seemed to sense his thoughts. "Don't worry," he said, "we need our martyrs to set a good example – it does us all good – stops us complaining when we feel hard done by."

"How many porters are there?" asked Francis.

"Fifteen, I think – two regular porters and twelve of us, including you – probably more on the way."

"How about the usual porters?"

"All called up of course – the Administrator was like hell about it – went right to the top apparently – asked them how he was supposed to run a hospital without porters – and d'you know what they said? – "Sorry we can't help – you'll have to solve that one yourself." Wish I could have been a fly on the wall – it must have been quite a moment. He was still fuming when he got back. I heard him telling the Head Porter that he'd have to ask the Ministry of Labour to get a move on and send some more of those so-and-so conchies immediately – no need for an interview – anything on two legs acceptable – I expect that's why they took you."

Francis remembered all the fuss at his tribunal, six weeks ago.

"Pity they couldn't have told everyone that there were hospital jobs going begging – it would have saved an awful lot of trouble."

"You don't really mean that, do you? Surely you must know that civil servants are singularly lacking in intelligence – they nearly always overlook the obvious."

"Who did you say was lacking in intelligence?" The Head Porter was standing by the door. Goodness knows how much he'd heard.

"Isn't it time you got back to X-ray?"

Giles looked at the clock. "Yes, I'm sorry – I should be there by now."

The Head Porter waited until he'd gone, then he phoned Casualty. "Could I speak to Staff, please? Yes, you'll be glad to hear that we have a new cleaner for you at last – yes, I'll bring him down now – straight away."

six

"Hello, Francis – your wife's on the phone, asking how you are. She sends her love and says she'll be up to see you as soon as we move you back to the main ward. She's still on the phone – is there anything you'd like to say to her?"

What on earth was she saying?

"Your wife – have you any messages for her?"

A strange voice, from far away. "Tell her I love her."

The footsteps receded and Francis tried to collect his thoughts. First of all, where was he? He forced himself to open his eyes and look around – more like a hotel room than a ward. The footsteps were returning, so he closed his eyes again to give himself more time to think.

> Francis had been wondering what he would probably be doing in Casualty ever since the voice of cold command had slammed the hatch in the porter's lodge. He had seen himself helping patients, reassuring them, lifting them out of ambulances, rushing them in on trolleys and generally making himself useful. But he now realised that this was not to be. Just cleaning and polishing. Never mind, that too was important and it was early days yet. Just being in Casualty would give him time to toughen up and become less squeamish.

> "Oh, there you are – you'll find your mop and pail in the sluice."
>
> Staff obviously had better things to do than waste time on a cleaner. Francis knew what a mop and pail

looked like, but he hadn't any idea what a sluice was – he'd have to ask a nurse.

"Excuse me – could you tell me where the sluice is?"
"Yes – over there."

The door said 'no admittance', but he took a chance and went in. He had to find his mop and pail. Perhaps there was a broom cupboard somewhere. The sluice was full of kitchen sinks and the taps had various messages and warning signs: hot only, cold only, drinking water only and – most mysterious of all – autoclave only. He was trying to work that one out when the door opened and Staff came in.

"You still here? Surely you can remember where you left your mop and pail?"

"Sorry, Staff – I'm new here – I don't know my way around yet."

She looked at him as though for the first time. "Of course you are – I remember now – the last cleaner couldn't stand the pace. It's quite straightforward really – all you have to do is to swab out Casualty each day, corners and all – quite easy if you keep at it." And she was gone again before he had a chance to say any more.

No broom cupboard in sight, but, heaven be praised, there was his wretched mop and pail, in the corner behind the sluice door, clearly visible to anyone except a congenital idiot. He filled the pail with hot water and mopped up the sluice, a trial run before he started in earnest. He didn't want people thinking he'd never done it before. Bad for the image.

He opened the door and sidled forth, mopping as he went.

"How about the middle bit?"

"I thought it would be easier to do that later, Staff, when you're not quite so busy."

"You must be joking – we're open twenty four hours a day here – there's a war on, remember?"

How could he forget, with a wretched mop and pail to keep him in his place? Never mind, he was getting the hang of it now. All he had to do was to keep going until he'd finished. It wasn't much to ask.

"Wake up, Francis. I've brought you a nice cup of tea."

So he must still be in hospital. So where? And why was he in a single room?

He opened his eyes and she smiled at him. A different nurse in a different uniform.

"I'm responsible for you for the next few days and another nurse will be responsible for you at night. We're never far away. All you have to do is to ring this bell and we'll be with you straight away. Would you like some breakfast?"

"I'm not sure," said Francis, "what have you got?"

"Anything you like."

Goody goody – this was better than a hotel.

"I'll have two eggs, bacon, mushrooms, fried bread, fried potato, toast and butter," he said.

The nurse laughed. "I can see you're feeling better already – perhaps a piece of bread and butter would be more appropriate – and would you like tea or coffee?"

He closed his eyes again. The feeble joke had taken it out of him, but it was his own fault – trying to make an impression, as usual.

The footsteps receded and he opened his eyes. It really was a lovely room, with a picture window overlooking some trees, with the country beyond. It was still quite early, but the sky was already blue, with fleecy, pink clouds – like cherubs, he thought, in a Pre-Raphaelite painting. He'd never seen pink clouds in the morning before. What a lovely sight. And how wonderful it was to be still alive.

The footsteps returned and he looked at her, really looked at her, for the first time – quite young, blue eyes and freckles. He'd always fancied freckles.

She put the tray down on his bedside table. "Here you are," she said. "I've brought you some porridge as a special treat and I'll stay with you while you eat it."

He looked up at her, gratefully.

"Do you feel like sitting up?" she asked.

It was only then that he saw all the tubes sticking into him. They had a depressing effect. "I don't think so, thank you," he said. "Perhaps tomorrow."

"Of course," she said. "It doesn't matter at all. I'll help you eat the porridge and you can drink your tea out of this special mug."

How kind she was.

"Where am I?" he asked between mouthfuls.

"You're in intensive care – this is where some patients come after their operations so that we can keep an eye on them."

"How long shall I be here?" he asked.

"That depends on you," she said. "The sooner you get better, the sooner you'll be able to go back to the ward – about a week if you behave yourself."

"No hurry," he said. "I'm beginning to enjoy myself here."

She smiled again – a frank, open smile.

"If you look out of the window," he said, "you'll see a lovely blue sky with pink clouds – aren't they lovely?"

"White clouds, actually," she said.

"Well, they were pink earlier on," said Francis. "I know you won't believe me, but they were a beautiful fleecy pink."

"How strange," she said. "I don't think I've ever seen pink clouds in the morning, but it's quite logical. The rising sun's just as likely to turn them pink in the morning as the setting sun is in the evening. Eat up now – the kitchen will want their tray back so they can wash up, but

I'll be back in five minutes and, if you still feel up to it, we can continue this stimulating conversation – or else you can go to sleep and I can gaze out of the window in the hope of seeing some pink clouds – even red, white and blue will do."

He was going to enjoy himself here. What a pity he'd have to leave in a few days.

The euphoria didn't last long. By lunchtime he was in agony and nurse had to fetch Sister, closely followed by two doctors. They stood at the bottom of his bed and conferred, just out of earshot. They looked at his notes and one of them gave Francis an injection.

"Hold still a moment – this will soon stop the pain."

The doctors left and Sister put in a new drip. Francis tried not to wince as the needle went in, but it certainly hurt. More than usual.

"Keep an eye on this patient, nurse – let me know if the pain comes back before you go off and I'll tell his night nurse to do something about it."

So I should jolly well hope, he thought.

He had a bad night and the night nurse eventually succumbed to his entreaties and gave him another injection.

> The first week was the worst. Francis lost track of the hours he worked each day, but he didn't mind. He opened his pay packet at the end of the week – his first ever pay packet – and counted out two pounds fifteen shillings, enough to pay for his bed and breakfast for the week, with enough over for a few pints at the local. He'd survived the first week and it would be easier from now on.
>
> "How's it going, old chap?"
>
> Giles had a girl with him. A pretty one, too, but he didn't introduce her.

"Not bad. I've survived – just – but I do miss Joanna."

"Funny you should say that – my friend here works in the Almoner's office and she told me that someone was leaving at the end of the month. There may be a chance for Joanna if you get a move on."

He wandered off to get a drink, leaving Francis to introduce himself.

She looked up at him and smiled. "I'm Peggy," she said. "He never introduces me to anyone."

"Yes, he is a bit casual, isn't he."

How attractive she was – short, curly hair and a magical smile.

"I couldn't help overhearing what you said just now – is Joanna your girl friend?"

"We were married six months ago."

"Lucky you."

"I would be if she was here with me. Perhaps we could afford to rent a flat or something if she could get a job up here."

"I heard that, too. Can she type?"

"Yes – she's a good touch typist."

"Right – the vacancy hasn't been advertised yet – I'll find out on Monday if they can interview her next week before the advert goes in and let you know. They pay three pounds ten a week, by the way."

"That's more than I'm getting."

She gave a wicked smile. "Touch typing is of course rather more skilled than scrubbing floors."

They burst out laughing. So Giles had told her, the swine. He'd get his own back one day.

They were still laughing when Giles returned.

"You two seem to be getting on well together."

"I hear you've been telling Peggy that I scrub floors for a living."

"I tell Peggy everything – or nearly everything."

"Not bad – you'll do."

It was Monday morning and Staff was doing the rounds. Nothing like a bit of praise to keep you going. Francis set to with a will and, by lunchtime, he'd managed to get as far as the corridor, so he leaned on his mop and watched the ebb and flow of patients, nurses, doctors, visitors and cleaners parading up and down, wondering where they were all going.

"I see you've settled in then."

God! – the gravelly voice of cold command. Francis spun round to see a pleasant looking young man, smiling at him. It couldn't possibly be him – or could it?

"Staff seems quite pleased with you – if you can please her you can probably please anyone. I'm the assistant administrator – thought I'd come by and see how you were getting on. We don't appear to have interviewed you yet – suppose it's a bit late, now you've started."

Sense of humour, too. Who would have thought it?

"We've got all your details upstairs in the office. Is there anything in particular you want to know?"

All sorts of things, really. "No sir – I don't think so – not at the moment, anyway."

"Well, if you think of anything you can always ask the head porter – he's been here a long time and he knows the ropes better than I do."

Modest, too. Strange how easy it was to misjudge people you hadn't met face to face.

"Thank you, sir."

Lunch break now. He had his sandwiches with him and he was looking forward to a cup of tea in the porter's rest room.

Giles was there before him. He usually was.

"Good news – Peggy's just told me. They haven't advertised the job yet and they'll be pleased to interview Joanna on Friday. The important thing is for you to get in touch with Joanna straight away and arrange to get her up here. What's her number?"

Giles really was a control freak, but a good friend and great in an emergency. He had written down the train times and Francis waited impatiently while he exchanged pleasantries with the operator. Francis snatched the phone away and heard the number ringing at last. He did so hope she'd be there, that she'd answer the phone herself. So much depended on it. . .

"Yes darling, it's me. Listen carefully – there may be a job for you here, in the hospital – in the Almoner's office. Can you come up on Friday for an interview? Good – suggest you catch the early train which gets here at mid-day – I'm not sure when it leaves your end, but please send me a telegram as soon as you can so that we know it's definite – must go now. . . I love you too."

The day had gone well and Francis met Giles and Peggy at the pub afterwards for a celebration.

"I've only just realised," said Giles, "that Peggy earns more than we do, so the drinks are on her this evening."

Peggy dutifully searched in her handbag and produced a five pound note.

"Hang on a second – I've never seen one of those before – you've been holding out on me."

"The difference between us," said Peggy, "is that I save my money, whereas you spend all yours on women and booze."

"That," said Giles, "is an unwarranted slur on my unimpeachable character."

"Doesn't he go on," said Peggy. "He'll get verbal indigestion if he's not careful."

"And another thing," said Francis, "he's a control freak as well."

They celebrated until closing time, then the three musketeers staggered home, arm in arm. Peggy's fiver had certainly come in handy.

seven

The doctors were there again when he woke up. The usual whispering, just out of earshot.

"We're going to give you another X-ray – no, don't worry – we're not going to move you, the radiographer will come to you – she'll be here in half an hour. No – no breakfast until we've seen the X-rays, but you may be able to have some lunch if you're lucky."

So that was that. Maybe he'd better go back to the main ward after all. At least they gave you something to eat from time to stop to stop you from dying of starvation.

"Sorry you're not feeling so well this morning."

His pretty little nurse with the freckles. How nice to have a bit of sympathy for a change.

"No – I've got this dreadful pain in my stomach – just there."

"Perhaps you ate too much yesterday."

Perhaps he did. Although, on second thoughts, all he had was some porridge.

"You mean old thing, you know perfectly well that all I had was a plate of porridge – you brought it to me yourself, and that was yesterday morning, twenty four hours ago."

"Never mind," she said, "perhaps the pain will go away if you keep quiet."

There came a tap on the door and the radiographer arrived with a huge machine on wheels. A very efficient, business-like radiographer. No nonsense with her around, that's for sure.

Nurse helped her set up, then she left the room while the radiographer did her stuff, then she came back again to help her pack up.

"Why did you leave the room nurse? You shouldn't have left me alone with a strange woman."

"You're incorrigible, you are. You know perfectly well that we all have to avoid unnecessary radiation."

"How about me? How about my radiation?"

"Oh, do be quiet, you do keep on so. I never know whether you're being serious or not, Now try to get some sleep and, if you're lucky, I may get you some tea when you wake up."

The builders were in when Francis arrived for work the next morning. The emergency doors were open and they were fitting a ramp over the steps. They already had a perfectly good double door with a ramp leading down to the ambulance park, so why bother with the emergency entrance, which was hardly ever used anyway?

He hadn't long to wait for the answer.

"Guess what?" said Giles at lunchtime. "We're on red alert."

Mr. Know-all again, how on earth did he get to know these things?

"There's been another raid on London and they're sending casualties further afield now. We're in line for the next lot – tomorrow probably."

"You must be kidding – they don't usually send ambulances all this way."

"Go and see for yourself – they're opening up the Nissen huts at the back of Casualty."

Sure enough, the two Nissen huts were swarming with workmen and electricians were checking the power points and fuses. The two regular porters were helping with the cleaning – the first time he'd seen them doing that – and Casualty Sister herself was keeping a watchful eye on the proceedings.

Francis carried on with his own cleaning, a process hampered somewhat by the delivery of twenty new beds from the stores. They were stacked neatly against the wall beside the emergency door and he suddenly resented the fact that he wasn't able to do something more useful.

"I quite agree with you," said Staff when he asked her. "The casualties should arrive late tomorrow, so take the morning off and come in after lunch, then stay tomorrow night. You'd better get a trolley and practice pushing it up and down the ramp as soon as it's ready. We don't want to lose too many patients on the way up, do we? I'm sure one of the nurses will be delighted to stand in as your patient while you learn."

It was the first time she had actually spoken to him as a person and Francis knew that he would be allowed, for the first time, to participate fully in what was going on. Now, which nurse did he fancy?

Francis had spotted a notice on the door of the porters' rest room that morning 'Emergency meeting – here – 1 p.m. – please come if you can. Signed Bill'. Bill was older than the rest of them and they had asked him to act as their spokesman with the hospital authorities if need be. He and his wife Rosina worked in the Dispensary. They were both qualified dispensing chemists and, as such, there had been no need for Bill to register as a conchie. But they were also Quakers, members of the Society of Friends, so Bill had naturally signed on as a conscientious objector. He had arrived as a porter and a porter he would remain. Rosina, on the other hand, had arrived as a dispensing chemist and her qualification enabled her to receive a monthly salary far greater than that of her husband. This enabled them to rent a nice large flat within easy walking distance of the hospital, where they were known for their kindness and hospitality.

Bill spoke first.

"Thanks for coming – eight of us – eight out of twelve, not bad. You probably all know that we're on red alert, which will mean overtime for everyone if a lot of casualties arrive. I saw the Administrator yesterday and he asked me to tell you this. We're here to discuss whether we should be paid for exceptional overtime or not. If you feel that we should, then he hopes you will all accept the same flat rate in the form of a bonus each week, but you may decide that, because we're all here as an alternative to military service, we should offer to do overtime without pay."

"How about the regular porters?" asked Pete.

Bill smiled. Pete had been a trade union organiser before the war.

"Don't worry about them," he said. "They have a good trade union, who negotiated their pay and their overtime long before the war, so our decision won't affect them."

He paused. "Any other comments? – Right, I suggest we have a show of hands. All those in favour of overtime during red alerts without extra pay? – Good, carried unanimously. By the way, nurses don't get paid for overtime either, so you'll be in good company. I didn't mention this before in case I was accused of trying to prejudice the vote. The meeting is now closed."

Francis was impressed. His first experience of democracy in action.

"Don't let it fool you," said Giles, "democracy only works when everyone agrees, more or less, with the proposal. If it had been anything really important we'd have been arguing here till midnight and we still wouldn't have been able to agree."

"Don't be such an old cynic – you're enough to put anyone off."

"Of course, it's my mission in life to persuade people not to be so stupid."

The meeting was over in ten minutes, so they sat around, eating their sandwiches and discussing the emergency.

"I feel almost sorry for the Administrator", said Bill, "having to employ a bunch of dissidents to run the hospital instead of regular porters who know what they're doing."

"Too many square pegs in round holes," said Francis.

Giles hesitated. "I haven't told you before, but I'm a first year medical student."

"So why on earth. . . " began Francis.

"Yes, I know. No need to register as a conchie – reserved occupation and all that – matter of principle I suppose – silly of me really."

So that's why he always seemed to be one jump ahead. Nothing like friends in high places. "Thanks for telling me," said Francis, "but surely you could help more as a medical student?"

"I doubt it," said Giles. "First year medical students spend most of their time attending lectures. I'm probably more useful in X-ray."

"Another martyr to the cause, I see."

Bill was smiling, supportively. He and Rosina were great. How comforting to be so sure that you were doing the right thing, thought Francis, when he himself and many of his new friends were still full of doubt and indecision.

eight

Tea was waiting, as promised, when Francis awoke.

"How about my X-Rays? Does this mean they're all right?"

"Ah, that would be telling. You'll have to wait until the doctor comes round this evening."

Another boring afternoon ahead. "How can I be expected to sleep with all these tubes stuck into me?"

No answer, so he turned over and went to sleep.

Nurse had gone off duty when he awoke and Sister was waiting for the night nurse to arrive.

"Ah, Francis," she said, "Mr Nandi will be coming to see you tomorrow morning, so the doctor won't be coming this evening. He'll be coming with Mr Nandi tomorrow."

"Who's Mr Nandi?" asked Francis.

"He's your surgeon – the one who did your operation. He will decide how long you should stay in intensive care, but you'll be here for another week at least. I'm sure you won't mind – it's much more comfortable here than in the main ward."

"Can I have something to eat, please?"

"I don't see why not – ask the night nurse when she arrives."

Mr Nandi had a sense of humour.

"I don't think much of your X-rays, but I suppose they're better than nothing. Now, what's all this about your terrible pain? Where does it hurt most?"

"My stomach, doctor."

"Let's have a look at you then... just as I thought, grossly overweight. Put this man on a diet, Sister. He'll never get better if he stays like this. I want him out of bed and exercising before he leaves here. There's nothing wrong with his stomach – nothing at all – but there soon will be if he stays in bed eating all day."

Francis started to protest, but thought better of it.

"If all goes well, we'll send you back to the ward at the end of the week and you'll be there for another two or three weeks after that. We're not out of the wood yet, but I expect you'll survive as long as you take plenty of exercise and don't eat so much."

It really was too much, having to put up with Mr Nandi, and Nurse grinning in the background.

"Right," she said, after Mr Nandi had gone, "no more whining about not having enough to eat – it's a strict diet for you from now on, whether you like it or not."

Francis got through the week somehow. He spent his nights dreaming that he was eating roast dinners instead of salad, but the pain in his stomach gradually got better and he sat out every day, grateful for the respite. The time came for him to say goodbye to his little nurse and she gave him a quick kiss.

"Don't go getting ideas," she said, "that was just a goodbye kiss – nothing more."

The porter came to take him back to the main ward and Francis could hardly wait to phone Joanna.

"Yes, I'm back in the main ward now – I'd love to see you... How soon can you come to see me?"

The telegram was waiting for Francis when he got back to his digs. It said, quite simply, 'Arriving Friday twelve noon please meet me at station love Joanna.' Francis read the telegram over and over again. She was coming to see him at last. How clever she was to get time off. How wonderful. How fantastic.

He could hardly wait to tell the others.

Giles, as usual, took charge. "Better make the appointment for 2 p.m. in case her train is late. Peggy will meet her at the station and bring her straight to the hospital."

Peggy started to say something, but Giles brushed her aside. He always did.

"Peggy can get time off easier than we can. They can take a taxi from the station and they'll be here in no time, then we can meet them both at the pub afterwards to celebrate."

Francis would have preferred Joanna to himself for a little while before her train left. "How about the red alert?" he asked.

"Probably a false alarm – they usually are – but, if it isn't, we'll be working all day tomorrow and tomorrow night, so they can hardly stop us leaving early on Friday, can they?"

They could of course, but it was no use telling Giles that. He'd only brush it aside.

"Peggy will write Joanna's name on a card and wait at the station until her train arrives. She'll probably be expecting Francis, but Peggy can always pretend to be a friend, so Joanna is bound to go with her – women are always curious about such things."

"Can I say something please?" Peggy was practically bursting.

"How dare you assume that women are interested in your arrogant assumptions. I've been sitting here listening to you telling Francis what you've arranged for me to do for quite long enough. Of course I'll meet Joanna at the station, but I'm certainly not going to be bossed around by you any more."

"Steady on old girl – I was only joking."

"I'm not your old girl – I'll have a large G&T please – and you can pay for the taxi on Friday."

Francis smiled to himself. Giles slunk off to the bar. He'd certainly met his Waterloo this time, serve him right, too.

"Wake up, lazybones."

He must have drifted off again. He'd been looking forward to seeing Joanna so much, too. He struggled to wake up, to listen to what she was saying.

"What do you mean? – sold my car." She'd actually gone ahead and sold his car, all by herself. Francis could almost see the car salesman, rubbing his hands in anticipation of a quick profit.

"How much did you get for it?" he asked, feebly. "How much? – you did what? – traded it in for what?"

He found it hard to believe – she'd done a deal with his old car, traded it in for a new car for herself and he could have her old car as soon as he was better, he could have her old wreck, waiting in the garage. It was all too much for one day – his lovely car, sunk without trace. Francis burst out laughing. What a fantastic thing to do.

CAR SALESMAN MEETS HIS WATERLOO –
DETERMINED WIFE SELLS HUSBAND'S CAR.

The real joke of course was the wreck in the garage instead of cash in the bank. She'd clipped his wings with a vengeance. She'd made absolutely sure that he wouldn't be able to drive until he was better.

"What a goose you are," she said. "You're either asleep or roaring with laughter." Her bright eyes were sparkling, the wrinkles wiped away as if by an unseen hand. She leaned forward and kissed him and they held hands for a long time, still laughing, giving one another strength until it was time for her to go.

Francis was still chuckling to himself when deep, untroubled sleep arrived, unannounced, and took over.

Arthur was still at the switchboard when Francis arrived the following morning.

"Thought you went off at seven," he said.

"So did I," said Arthur, "I usually do, but it's been a hell of a night. The ambulances arrived at last, all ten of them – must have been about midnight, only twenty minutes warning, too. I phoned Casualty direct and warned them, then I tried to contact Admin., but no one there of course – too much to expect them to give up their beauty sleep. So I phoned round most of the other departments and warned them too – then the phones started ringing and I've been at it ever since – people anxious about their relatives, asking for information. Casualty had a list of names, but that's about all. I tried ringing the Nissen huts, but the phones there weren't working, so I couldn't get anywhere – asked everyone to ring again in the morning, when we should be able to give them more information – and so on and so on, all night long. Haven't even been able to stop for a cup of tea – ah, here they are, on time for a change."

The two regular telephonists had arrived, giggling as usual.

"Hear you had a nice quiet night, Arthur."

"See what I mean? No one appreciates the night shift, never have done. Anyway, I'm off now – just in time for breakfast."

Francis hurried down the corridor to Casualty. He met Staff, just going off and looking the worse for wear – she must have been up all night. He gave her a grin and she gave him a tired smile, but her voice was firm.

"Sister wants to see you as soon as you arrive – go straight to her office."

What had he done now? Sister had never asked to see him before – in fact he doubted whether she even knew about him.

He knocked on Sister's door.

"Ah, come in Francis and sit down. These two officers will be helping us for the next few weeks. They will be working as ward orderlies in the Nissen huts and the three of you will take patients to Theatre and X-ray."

Francis saw that they were in uniform – Royal Army Medical Corps. They must have arrived with the casualties last night.

"You'd better wear these white coats for the time being – leave your jackets here – you too Francis."

Nothing like an emergency, he thought. Double promotion overnight, from cleaner to porter to ward orderly, all in one go – can't be bad.

"Report to me before you leave so that I know what's going on."

They opened the emergency door and stood at the top of the ramp, where workmen were fixing a new handrail and putting the final touches to a makeshift roof. As they stood there, a post office van drew up and an engineer got out.

"Someone's reported a line fault – this sort of thing always happens when builders are around."

"That's right – pick on us. If you lot did your stuff properly to begin with, you wouldn't have to keep barging in and blaming us for your rotten workmanship."

The fault was quickly repaired, and the van drove away leaving a bedraggled newspaper blowing fitfully in its wake.

HAND TO HAND FIGHTING IN STALINGRAD

> Thousands of civilians are dead after months of savage and bloody street fighting. The gallant Russian defenders of Stalingrad continue their desperate resistance against overwhelming odds. Red Army survivors lie low by day and attack the Nazi invaders by night. The German tanks which have been bombarding continuously from the west bank of the Volga have almost run out of fuel and are critically short of ammunition.

STALINGRAD NO LONGER A TOWN

A *Reuters* report from Moscow received yesterday contains graphic extracts from a letter written by a German officer of the 24th Panzer division shortly before his capture: 'Stalingrad is no longer a town. By day it is an enormous cloud of burning, blinding smoke – a vast furnace lit by the reflection of flames. And, when night arrives, escaping dogs plunge into the Volga and swim desperately to gain the other bank.'

SCENES FROM HELL

Thousands of blackened corpses, friend and foe, together at last in death, lie in piles, waiting for burial, but the hatred of those still alive is so intense that very few prisoners are taken, neither is there any chance of a temporary truce to bury their dead. The nightmare that is now Stalingrad is a terrible condemnation of the ferocity of the brutal hand to hand fighting which may well mark the beginning of the end for Nazi Germany.

nine

Francis turned to his new colleagues.

"I'm Francis," he said.

"I'm Bruno," said the older one, burly and efficient-looking, "and my friend here is Alfonso."

Francis hesitated.

"I know – Italian names, aren't they, but don't let that worry you – we're on your side."

"How did you come to be here?"

"We are – or rather were – first year medical students and we were studying in London when the war started, so we became enemy aliens and had to go before a tribunal. There was always the possibility that we would be interned for the duration of the war, but they suggested that we might like to join the Royal Army Medical Corps and put our training to good use. So we did – and here we are."

"Why here?" asked Francis.

"We were due for a spot of leave, but they asked for volunteers to accompany the ambulances from London yesterday and Alfonso discovered that his uncle was a casualty on this lot, so we asked to come here. His uncle is not all that bad – he's tucked up nicely in one of the Nissen huts, so we'll go and visit him as soon as the coast is clear."

What a strange world, thought Francis. Here we are, an odd assortment of friends, enemies, conchies, army conscripts and even first year medical students, all thrown together, doing our best to help the hospital run as efficiently as possible despite the extra problems caused by the war. He was suddenly proud of what he was doing He was learning now how to help people in hospital more effectively and he didn't have to apologise to himself or to anyone else for being a conchie – anyone who didn't like it could get stuffed.

They spent an hour or so cleaning up Casualty, helping the nurses bin the bloodstained bandages ready for Ray's next visit and lining up the spare beds delivered by stores for use in the new wards. It didn't take Francis long to realise how very well organised Bruno and Alfonso were and how well they worked together. Army training and army discipline had obviously been very effective in their case. They seemed to get through twice as much work as he did without any apparent effort and he had to work doubly hard to keep up with them. They knew how to lift patients and make them more comfortable and the nurses were glad of their help. Francis watched them at work and Bruno in particular encouraged him to overcome his initial shyness.

"Another few months and you won't need us any more," he said with a grin.

The builders had more or less finished, so they each took a trolley and pushed through the emergency exit, down the ramp and up the path to the first Nissen hut, where a staff nurse was waiting for them.

"About time, too. I've a patient here, asking for Alfonso."

"That's me," said Alfonso.

"Last bed on the left – you two, come with me."

She led the way into the office.

"You're Bruno, I believe – and you must be Francis. Sit down for a moment and tell me what you know."

"Not much really," said Bruno, modestly. "I'm a first year medical student and I've had some ward experience, lifting, simple diagnosing, even a few injections, making myself generally useful and learning at the same time."

"How about you?" she asked Francis.

"I'm afraid I don't know anything," said Francis, apologetically.

"I thought you were a ward orderly."

"Not really – just a porter."

Staff gave him a friendly smile.

"Never mind," she said. "There's plenty of trolley work to Theatre and X-ray and a nurse will go with you for the time being. Now let's see how Alfonso is getting on."

Alfonso was sitting on his father's bed and Francis saw that he had tears in his eyes. He was smaller than Bruno and more emotional. Francis envied Italians, people who didn't need and weren't expected to keep a stiff upper lip. Emotions, he thought, were meant to be shared, not bottled up. How sensible to cry when you felt like it. And the way they embraced one another, how natural it all was.

The Nissen huts were joined together by a corrugated iron archway. They were only a few feet apart, so, with a wooden floor and plasterboard walls, the archway turned the two huts into a perfectly acceptable ward. The patients in the next hut were mostly sitting up and there were only a few beds. Staff led the way.

"The chair cases have to go to Casualty this afternoon – there's a special ear clinic at 2 pm, so don't be late back after lunch – in fact you'd better go to lunch now."

Francis took Bruno and Alfonso to the porter's rest room for a pot of tea and they shared their sandwiches.

"What's an ear clinic?" asked Francis. "Why do they all have to go?"

"Blast," said Bruno. "Most air raid casualties are affected by blast – it perforates the outer ear membrane and deposits quite a lot of debris in the middle ear – dust particles and so on. These particles have to be removed carefully to avoid long term damage to the ear drum – sometimes quite painful, as the patient has to be conscious while this is being done. The clinic this afternoon is to assess the extent of the damage before they start digging out the debris and a preliminary assessment usually takes about ten minutes for each patient."

The clinic finished on time and the patients were all back in the ward by six o'clock. Staff was impressed.

"I hope I haven't worked you too hard."

"Not at all, Staff. See you tomorrow."

Francis stayed behind. He'd better ask her now while she was in a good mood.

"Would it be possible for me to leave at four o'clock tomorrow afternoon?"

"Any particular reason?"

"Yes, Staff, my wife is coming up tomorrow for an interview and she has to catch the six o'clock train home. I'd like to spend an hour with her before she leaves."

"Of course, Francis. What's her name?"

Strange question. "Joanna, Staff."

"Wasn't it a bit risky, getting married?"

"What do you mean – risky?"

"No, I didn't mean that. I was only wondering what would have happened if your exemption was refused and you had to go to prison. It wouldn't have been very nice for her to have a jailbird for a husband, let alone one who is a conscientious objector. Conscientious objectors are hardly the flavour of the month, are they? And how about her family? What do they think about it?"

"They're not at all pleased," said Francis.

"Well then – I admire you both for what you're doing. My father was a conscientious objector in the last war and he had a pretty rough time of it. Stick to what you believe in."

Fancy that! Something welled up inside him – gratitude? relief? joy? It was more than that – a feeling that, all around, the most unexpected people shared his beliefs, difficult in the middle of a bitter war, but the support was there and it surfaced every now and then, often when least expected.

"Thank you, Staff – and goodnight."

ten

"Right – up you get."

Realisation came swiftly, like a bucket of cold water.

He was back in the main ward and they were bugging him already.

Francis yawned and opened his eyes. No breakfast yet, either.

"Time to get out of bed and sit in your chair – breakfast will be here shortly."

He didn't really feel like breakfast, in fact he didn't feel like getting up either.

"I don't feel very well," he said, apologetically.

He stayed in bed and drank a cup of tea, while his porridge congealed.

The porter came to take him to X-ray, the same porter who had been fetching him from the intensive care unit every morning. Dr. Nandi was still insisting on daily X-rays for his heart and lung bypass patients.

"Nearly went to ICU to collect you this morning – just shows what creatures of habit we are, but what can you expect from such a boring job?"

Francis remembered his three years as a hospital porter. "You're quite right," he said, "it is a bit boring."

"What d'you know about it? People like you don't know what it's like, pushing a trolley all day."

"Yes I do," said Francis, "I pushed a trolley for three years during the war."

The porter looked at him, curiously.

"Were you one of those, what do you call 'em, conscience objectors?"

"Yes – that's right," said Francis.

"My dad was in the war," said the porter. "He didn't care much for it, either."

Another X-ray over and done with, that made eight in all. Francis had hardly got back to the ward when Sister spied him.

"Time for physiotherapy now – I'll send a porter to take you."

"Sorry Sister – I don't feel up to it this morning." And he really didn't.

"Very well – if it's too much effort for you to go to the physiotherapist, she'll have to come to you."

He lay there, too weak to protest, waiting for the onslaught.

She came almost immediately, a vicious little creature in a white coat, with cold, fishy eyes. She made him lie on his stomach and pummelled him mercilessly until he cried out in agony.

"Don't be such a baby. It's your own fault – you should have come to physio at the same time as the others."

Just as he thought – she was punishing him – getting her own back, just because she had to come to him, showing off in front of Sister. He hated her, frustrated little bitch. He hated everyone, the whole, bloody hospital. The pain was so intense that his ears buzzed and he knew he was going to faint, but she still carried on until everything went black. . .

    Francis was in the pub with Peggy.
    "Where's Giles?"
    "Oh, he's gone off somewhere – never tells me anything."

She sounded a bit despondent and obviously needed cheering up. Perhaps a gin and tonic would do the trick.

"Couple of handsome Italians joined us this morning – they're here to help with the casualties and I've been told to join them. So I've been promoted to ward orderly for the time being – not that I know what I'm meant to be doing, mind you, but they're short of staff, so I suppose it's a case of any port in a storm."

She laughed. She was so pretty when she laughed.

"All set for tomorrow morning?"

"Yes, fine – I'm taking the day off. Have you got a photo of Joanna?"

"Don't lose it, will you," he said as he handed it over.

"My – isn't she pretty – hardly surprising you wanted to marry her – wonder what on earth she saw in you?"

"My character, of course, coupled with my good looks and fantastic personality."

She laughed again and he went on to relate the events of the day, how Alfonso's uncle was a patient and how fond they were of each other.

"The old chap must be feeling lonely – Italians are very family orientated and I don't expect his relatives know where he is yet. Alfonso and his friend Bruno are both first year medical students – they joined the RAMC so that they wouldn't be interned – quite sensible, really."

"No wonder you can't keep up with them."

They left early and he walked her home, arm in arm.

"Thanks for cheering me up," she said. Then she suddenly reached up and kissed him, full on the mouth.

"That's to be going on with," she said, "until Joanna gets here."

Friday morning and the sweet taste of Peggy's unexpected kiss still lingered. Things had settled down in the new ward and they were having a cup of coffee.

"Alfonso, your uncle has a visitor – would you like to come and meet her?"

"Who would visit him, Staff? He doesn't know anyone here except me."

"You'd better come and translate," said Staff. "I'm sure she'd like to meet you, too."

Alfonso soon returned. "A beautiful girl has come," he said. "She'd like to meet Bruno and Francis as well."

It was Peggy of course, looking prettier than ever, with a huge bunch of flowers for Alfonso's uncle. The old man was grasping her hand as if he'd never let go, his eyes full of tears.

"I wanted to meet you as well," she said to Bruno, "you're Alfonso's friend, aren't you?"

Alfonso couldn't take his eyes off her. Love at first sight, thought Francis. How irrational – and how annoying – that he himself should feel feel so jealous.

They talked for a while, then Peggy looked at her watch.

"Good heavens," she said. "I've got a train to catch and I've got a taxi waiting outside."

Francis was astonished. "Not a taxi? Surely you haven't kept it waiting all this time?"

"Don't worry," she said. "Giles is taking care of the taxi – remember what he said? – besides, he's got more money than you think. I'm off to meet Joanna now. See you in the pub about half past four."

A glimpse of sunlight on golden hair and she was gone. The ward suddenly seemed empty.

"Isn't it time you stopped mooning over that girl and thought about work for a change? Bruno, you help nurse prepare Mr Caldrose for Theatre – he's already had his pre-med. Francis, take him to Theatre when he's ready. Nurse will go with you – he's on a drip, so be careful. Alfonso, stay with your uncle for a while – you both seem quite overcome at the moment."

Francis was impressed, she hadn't been made staff nurse for nothing. He set out for Theatre, patient on trolley, nurse by his side. He'd never been to the operating theatres before and he hadn't any idea which way to go, but he strode on confidently. Direction signs always disappeared when they were most needed. The corridors were endless and he was soon completely lost.

"Shouldn't we have gone that way?" asked the nurse.

"Really?" said Francis. "I prefer this way myself, but perhaps your way is quicker."

"I'm not sure," said the nurse, uncertainly.

"You may be right, come to think of it – we'll go your way."

"You sure you don't mind?"

"Not at all – now, do we have to go back?"

"No – first left will do – it joins up with the main corridor and leads straight to Theatre."

Thank goodness for her sense of direction.

"Well done, Francis." Staff was waiting for him. "The others have gone to lunch – hope you didn't get lost."

"Of course not, Staff, but I did come back the long way to familiarise myself with the rest of the hospital in case you wanted me to visit the canteen at any time."

Risky, but it paid off.

"I'm glad to know you have a sense of humour, Francis. Now off to lunch with you and don't forget you're leaving early this afternoon."

As if he could. Only three hours to go and he'd be with her at last. He could hardly wait to see her smile as she welcomed him, so much to talk about and so little time. But it was better than nothing. She'd be in the Almoner's office now, waiting for her interview. So much depended on it. Perhaps they'd let her know straight away.

He didn't feel like going to the rest room, he'd have to listen to Giles and Bruno and Alfonso talking about their first year experiences, way over his head, so he went outside to eat his sandwiches. It was a lovely September afternoon and the trees in the garden were turning russet brown. He felt a longing for peace, a longing for the countryside. When this was all over, they'd live somewhere in the country and be together all the time.

"Ah, Francis!" He knew from the tone of her voice that Staff had a job for him. What a nuisance he'd got back from lunch so early.

"Glad you know where the canteen is. Here's a pound – go and get some cakes and we'll make tea for the visitors – they'll be arriving about half past two. I'll make the tea and you can be tea boy."

Never a dull moment.

"How many visitors?" he asked.

"How should I know? Get as many cakes as you can – and don't forget the change."

The visitors were starting to arrive when he returned. They stood, awkwardly, just inside the door, not knowing where to go, then they gradually gained confidence and walked around until they found who they were looking for. Tired eyes lit up in love and recognition, kisses were exchanged and grapes and flowers appeared, then the visitors paused, not knowing what to do next. They needed time to adjust – to find the right words for the occasion. They looked around for chairs, then they sat down gently, smiling at each other, producing oranges from paper bags. They admired the flowers and talked about the weather. They were strangers in a strange land, unsure of themselves, feeling almost guilty at being there.

"Tea up." Staff knew a thing or two about making visitors feel at home.

Francis wheeled in the tea trolley, cakes piled high. The transformation was instant.

"How kind of you – and what lovely cakes."

Staff chatted to the visitors, reassuring them, answering their questions and Francis poured out the tea, listening to her, full of admiration – what a wonderful nurse she was.

"Time to go, Francis."

He looked at his watch – four o'clock on the dot. Of course, Joanna would be waiting for him. Staff never missed a trick.

eleven

"Good God, man – haven't you seen his X-rays? Take a look at this!"

Mr Nandi himself. By the sound of it, his usual bedside manner somewhat strained.

"Nurse – fetch a trolley – we'll have to drill him out where he is, straight away."

Something bored into his side, low down.

"You have to be careful while you're doing this – too low and you're in trouble."

Francis struggled to say something – it sounded like 'How about the poor patient? He's the one in trouble.'

He opened his eyes and the great man actually smiled at him. Something was definitely wrong.

"Got it at last."

The smell was overpowering, but the tube was in, doing its stuff, draining the poison from his lung until he could breathe freely again.

Francis lay quite still, taking deep breaths, filling his lungs with air. How wonderful to be alive, to be able to breathe, to relax, to sleep.

Francis met Giles in the corridor.

"Come on – I've been waiting here for ages. Joanna will have arrived by now. She's your wife, remember, not mine – don't want to keep her waiting."

Self righteous as usual, but never mind. The pub was only a brief walk away. Francis was nearly there, only another hundred yards and then, and then. . . He burst through the door and there she was – more beautiful than ever – the same luminous eyes, the same shy smile. His heart was bursting as they hugged each other, oblivious to everything except themselves. She was crying now and he wasn't far behind, but he managed to collect his thoughts.

"This is Giles," he said, "he's a good friend – you've already met Peggy."

"Of course I have, you goose – I wouldn't be sitting here but for her."

The girls were obviously good friends already.

"You might like to know," said Peggy, "that while we've been waiting for you we've nearly been picked up – twice."

Francis gave Peggy a kiss. "Thanks for everything," he whispered.

Giles gave Joanna a kiss and the barman brought the champagne.

"Whatever's this?" they chorused, knowing full well.

Giles preened himself. "Thought we needed something worthy of the occasion."

They drank a toast to Joanna, then Francis just had to know.

"The interview," he asked. "How did it go?"

"I'm not sure", said Joanna, but the girls were giggling by now.

"I'm not sure about the interview," she said. "But I've got the job."

They'd planned to keep it as a secret for a little while longer, but he was glad they hadn't, the suspense would have been unbearable. Now at last he could relax and enjoy himself.

"Let's go to the bar, Giles, and get another drink."

Peggy of course, intuitive as usual, giving them time to themselves. It was five o'clock now – time to finish the champagne, then twenty minutes to the station by taxi and another twenty minutes before the train left.

They held hands and gazed at each other, not moving, not speaking. Just content to have this beautiful moment – a moment to savour.

"When do you start?" he asked.

"Three weeks," she said. "We'll have to find somewhere to live."

"Don't worry," he said, "leave that to me."

"I don't have much choice, do I?"

"I suppose not." They both laughed and he knew then that she wasn't worried.

"How about your family?" he asked.

"They don't know why I'm here – they think I've just come up to see you."

"And so you have – and you just happened to find a job while you were here."

They laughed again.

"What do they think about us? Have they forgiven you for marrying me yet?"

"I don't think so – we never talk about it."

"Drink up then – we have to go soon – there's a taxi waiting."

Good old Giles, everything arranged as usual.

"Peggy and I will come with you in the taxi and drop you off at the station, then we'll come back here to drown our sorrows."

They drank up and piled into the taxi. They didn't say much on the way and even Peggy and Joanna had stopped giggling, only too aware that the moment of departure was at hand.

"Goodbye, dear," said Peggy, "I'm so glad you got the job – we'll be meeting again in three weeks – not long, really."

"Goodbye Peggy, goodbye Giles – and thank you so much for all you've done."

Twenty minutes to go. They found an empty carriage and clung together desperately, knowing she had to go, counting the minutes before she left. The whistle blew and, with a final hug, Francis opened the carriage door and stood on the platform, forlorn and miserable.

"Don't worry," shouted Joanna as the porter closed the door. "Just think, we'll be together for good in another three weeks."

Francis watched as the train gathered speed. How lucky he was to be seeing her again so soon. There must be hundreds of thousands of couples saying goodbye to each other all over Europe, not knowing whether they would ever see each other again. How lucky he was.

twelve

The vicious little creature was at it again, but more gently this time, her cold, fishy eyes almost friendly. Encouraged by her half smile, Francis plucked up the courage to ask her what the trouble was .

"Empyema," she said. "I'm afraid you have empyema."

"What's that?" he asked, but she had already reverted to type.

"For goodness sake, stop talking and concentrate on your breathing."

Francis, who had been breathing quite nicely before she started, decided that he hated her as much as ever.

"What's empyema?" he asked Sister as soon as fisheyes had gone.

Sister didn't tell him either, but she was as sweet as pie and even the ECG man tried to raise a smile. People were actually being nice to him, so something must be seriously wrong. Perhaps they thought he was a private patient; he didn't even have to ask for fish – it just came, on a special plate. And very nice it was too. His mouth was full of fish when the executioner arrived.

"Would you like to sign this?"

"Sign what?"

"Just the usual consent form – we're going to insert a small tube in your lung."

"Whatever for?" asked Francis, "I've already got one, quite low down."

The executioner looked at his assistant.

"We have to take the old tube out," he said, patiently, "and put a new tube in, further up."

"How do you get it in?" asked Francis, suspiciously.

The executioner sighed. "It's quite a small operation – we remove about five inches of rib and put the new tube in – you won't feel a thing.

"I should hope not," said Francis.

The executioner grinned, reassuringly. "Just sign this, there's a good chap."

Francis signed his life away with a flourish and carried on eating his fish. Things weren't so bad after all.

> Francis walked slowly back to the pub. Joanna's brief visit had only served to remind him how lonely he was and he was glad to find Giles and Peggy still there. Peggy had bought a local paper and she was busy sifting through the accommodation section.
>
> "Three or four possibles here – we'll go round the estate agents tomorrow and get details. Saturday afternoon should be a good time to make a start."
>
> Giles seemed less enthusiastic.
>
> "I'm afraid I can't make it tomorrow – I have to go to tea with my mother."
>
> Poor Peggy, so full of enthusiasm, but so little response from Giles. Francis knew that without her help he wouldn't stand a chance of finding anything suitable.
>
> They traipsed around the estate agents the next day, listening to sales talk and collecting details of three likely lets. They visited all three, only to find them scarcely fit for human habitation and, discouraged, decided to call it a day.
>
> "Let's have a cup of tea," said Francis. "I think we deserve one after all this."

She looked at him, gratefully, and they went to a little café up a side street. They pushed open the door and a little bell rang, a tinkling sound. There was a rustle of disapproval from the other customers and, after a while, a distressed gentlewoman appeared.

"Good afternoon – would you like to sit over there?"

They sat over there.

"Would you like the afternoon tea or the cream tea?"

The assembled multitude held their breaths. Which was it to be?

"Could we just have a pot of tea and some biscuits?"

Consternation all round.

"I'm afraid we only do afternoon teas or cream teas. I'm so sorry."

They looked at each other and Peggy started to laugh.

"We'll just have the ordinary tea," said Francis, spluttering.

"I'm afraid we don't do ordinary teas – only afternoon teas or cream teas."

"Just the afternoon tea," said Francis, hysterically.

The rustle of disapproval intensified, but nothing could drown their laughter. They tried to stifle it, but this only made matters worse. The tears ran down their cheeks at the sheer absurdity of it all. They were still laughing when the distressed gentlewoman reappeared with the afternoon tea and began to arrange the china teapot, the cups and saucers, the milk jug, the hot water jug, the tea strainer, the serviettes, the teaspoons, the sugar and the sugar tongs with military precision.

"Thank goodness we didn't have the cream tea – we'd have been here all the afternoon," whispered Peggy. "She might even have died of old age before she'd finished laying the table – and then where would we be?"

They started laughing all over again and the rustle of disapproval rose to a crescendo. They tried to drink their tea, but it splashed all over the tablecloth. No wonder young people were viewed with such suspicion – they really couldn't behave themselves – they should be prevented from having afternoon tea until they were old enough to behave properly.

They left two shillings on the table – that should cover it – and beat a hasty retreat before the distressed gentlewoman could return and start them laughing all over again.

So much for house hunting: no lunch, because of Giles, and no tea, because of unforeseen circumstances.

"Tell you what," said Francis, "we'll stuff ourselves with fish and chips, then we'll go to the pub and wash it down."

"Good idea." Peggy was still giggling. "I haven't laughed so much for ages. We must go there again sometime."

They spent the evening in the pub. Saturday night was a good night for pubbing, you could always rely on meeting someone you knew.

"I wonder who we shall meet this evening?" Peggy, ever the extrovert, looked around.

"How about those two at the bar? I'm sure I've seen them before."

She certainly had. Bruno and Alfonso were propping up the bar, singing Italian songs to an increasingly hostile audience. The presence of Italians singing Italian songs in an English pub while England was at war with Italy was risky in the extreme, particularly on a Saturday night.

"Wait here." Francis thought later that he'd probably only just managed to rescue them in time to prevent an ugly incident. He bought them each a drink and shepherded them towards the table by the window. Peggy would keep them out of mischief – and he was right – they could hardly wait to start flirting with her.

"How's your uncle?" asked Peggy, doing her best to keep her distance.

Alfonso slid closer. "When can we meet again?" he asked, passionately.

"Your uncle," she asked, "how is he?"

"He's fine," said Alfonso, absently.

Bruno intervened. "He's not all that well," he said. "He'll be all right eventually, but he'll have to stay in hospital for at least another week."

"This is Nurse Jarrett," said Sister. "She knows all about empyema and she'll tell you about the small operation you'll be having first thing tomorrow morning."

Talk about VIP treatment. Nurse Jarrett was an absolute beauty.

"I'm looking after you and Mr Curry tonight – you'll both be having the same operation and you'll be isolated from the other patients for the time being. Empyema is quite contagious, so we don't want anyone else to have it, do we?"

Nurse Jarrett smiled, an angelic smile, and plunged a syringe into his thigh. He'd been on the point of dozing off, but he shot up in bed, wide awake.

"Glad to see you looking so well," she said, cheerfully. "Just relax – you'll soon be asleep."

Francis was trying to work out the logic of waking people up to give them injections to put them to sleep, when he suddenly saw Nurse Jarrett floating in the air, smiling at him, beckoning him to follow. . . They were floating away on a magic carpet, up through the cold night air, over the Alps and down into Persia, with the desert beneath them. The desert was strewn with rocks and boulders and she was lying there, waiting for him, with her milky white thighs and breasts like water melons. She held out her arms and he tried, desperately, to reach her, but the rocks and boulders kept getting in the way. She was laughing at him now, teasing him, and his back was aching. . .

Sunday morning.

"Phone call for you, Francis."

"Joanna, dear. . ."

"No – it's Peggy. Sorry to disappoint you, but my mother knows someone who lives on the Common – number ten. She has a lovely large house and a flat upstairs – fully furnished, with its own entrance at the side of the house. Sounds ideal if you can get it at the right price – she suggests we might like to go and see it this afternoon."

"Sounds great – shall I meet you there?"

"Hang on a sec. I'll ask my mother. That's fine – how about three o'clock?"

Three o'clock it was and she was already there. She was wearing a powder blue coat and she looked absolutely stunning.

"How lovely you look to-day." It was the first time he'd paid her a direct compliment and she looked embarrassed for a moment, but recovered immediately. "Don't look so bad yourself, considering."

They rang the bell and a tall, distinguished looking lady opened the door.

"So you're Peggy – and this. . . ?"

"Is my friend, Francis. His wife is coming up to join him in three weeks' time and Giles and I are trying to help them find suitable accommodation."

The lady obviously knew Giles, perhaps she was his mother. Francis dismissed the thought, but he still sensed a slight embarrassment on Peggy's part, perhaps because she realised that the posh lady might be wondering why she – Peggy – was helping him find a flat instead of his own wife. Perhaps, even, wondering why they were here without Giles.

Peggy intercepted the thought. "Giles couldn't come to-day – he's not very well."

"Sorry to hear that, dear. Now let me show you round."

So Peggy had told a lie – a deliberate lie – to cover her embarrassment. Peggy, of all people, covering up so that the posh lady wouldn't discover the truth. Perhaps she even fancied him after all. Francis had always fancied her, but that was different. This could be more complicated. She was great fun to be with and he enjoyed flirting with her, but that was all.

It was certainly a lovely flat – bedroom, living room, kitchen and bathroom, all beautifully furnished, with stairs leading down to the front hall and a side entrance.

"I expect she'll want a fiver at least," whispered Peggy.

Francis made a lightning calculation: his pay two pounds fifteen shillings, plus Joanna's three pounds ten shillings, total six pounds five shillings. No, his original calculations were correct: they couldn't afford more than three pounds a week maximum. Pity, it would have suited them perfectly.

"I was thinking of five or six pounds a week," said the posh lady. "Have another look round and let me know tomorrow. I've got visitors arriving any moment so I'll have to go now, but stay for a while and have a look round if you like. Let yourselves out through the side door and don't forget to pull it to behind you when you leave."

Francis and Peggy stood in the bedroom and looked at the gorgeous double bed. Then, like kids, they jumped on the bed and bounced up and down.

They suddenly found themselves in each other's arms. They cuddled each other, shivering with desire, then Peggy broke away, threw off her coat and unbuttoned her blouse. Francis buried his head between her breasts, her beautiful, pointed breasts. Then he too undressed and she lay on top of him, fitting him gently between her legs, moving slowly up and down, then with increasing ferocity until they both climaxed. She was more experienced than Joanna and he loved the way she took the initiative. It was exciting with her on top and he fondled her continuously to add to their pleasure, then they rolled over and gazed at each other in awe.

"What have we done?" asked Peggy, aghast.

"I don't know what you've done, but I can't help loving you, now more than ever. I shall always remember to-day."

"Me too," said Peggy, "though it musn't happen again – ever. I'm very fond of Joanna and I wouldn't do anything to hurt her."

They lay together for a while, then they got up, went downstairs and let themselves out through the side door. They walked back through the park in silence, stopping from time to time to kiss, long, lingering, farewell kisses in memory of a moment that would never come again.

thirteen

"Careful with that tube, nurse."

It was Mr Curry in the next bed, lying on his stomach with a tube sticking out of his back. The wretched fellow had spoilt it all. Typical of him, thought Francis, paradise never lasted with people like him around – never even started, for that matter.

"How's it going, then?"

Mr Curry grinned – a friendly, toothless smile – and Francis saw that they shared a common fate. He too was lying on his stomach and almost certainly had a tube sticking out of his back.

"When did they do it?" he asked.

"No idea, mate – that nurse gave me a Mickey Finn, just like yours, and I woke up to find this bleeding tube sticking out of me back."

Francis felt, gingerly, between his shoulder blades and, sure enough, it was there. Perhaps their tubes would have to stay there for ever, sticking up like periscopes for the rest of their lives.

> FOR SALE – VINTAGE ROBOTS,
> GOING CHEAP. LUBRICATION – GIN & TONIC.
> SERVICING – OVERNIGHT, TWICE WEEKLY –
> OFFERS INVITED.

"Beats me what you find to laugh about."

How on earth could he explain, they lived in different worlds, the tubes their only shared experience.

"How long d'you think we're going to be like this?" he asked.

"Don't ask me, mate – 'aven't a clue – wish I could 'ave a fag."

Perhaps the smoke would emerge from his tube when he puffed, useful for sending messages. One puff for a bottle, two for a bedpan, three for a nurse, four for a letter, five for something better. Ten puffs would signal the Indian uprising – the downtrodden patients would leap from their beds, butcher the doctors, torture the physiotherapists, tie matron to a stake and rape the nurses. Not all of them of course, just the pretty ones. The others would be forced to eat the entire contents of the dinner trolley – congealed fat, lumps of grease, stale vegetables – the lot.

Francis suddenly vomited.

"Now look what you've done – all over the bed, too."

"Sorry, nurse."

"So I should hope – can't think why you can't control yourself – you're not a baby, you know, so try not to behave like one."

Francis made a mental note to deal with her personally when the time came.

> Giles was waiting for Francis in the porter's rest room when he arrived on Monday.
>
> "What's all this about my being ill? My aunt rang up yesterday – very concerned she was, too."
>
> So the posh lady was his aunt, was she? What a coincidence.

"It's your fault for not coming with us," said Francis. "She seemed to think it rather strange that you weren't with us yesterday."

"How on earth could I be when I didn't even know you were going?"

"You knew perfectly well we were flat hunting on Saturday and you left us to it – remember? Anyway, your aunt kept on asking where you were, so Peggy said you were ill to shut her up. Sorry about that, but it's your own fault."

Giles, for once, was reduced to silence. The best method of defence was obviously attack – he must remember that in future.

He didn't see Peggy for three days. It seemed like a lifetime. He haunted the pub every evening, hoping for a glimpse of her, perhaps a smile – anything to reassure him that they were still friends. Bruno and Alfonso called in every evening, but they didn't stay long. And then it happened.

"Hello Frankie."

Joy of joys – it was her, but why Frankie?

"Makes a change – it's more masculine somehow."

"What d'you mean, more masculine?"

"Don't know, really – it's just that I've recently had first hand experience of your masculinity – isn't that enough?"

She gave a wicked grin.

Good old Pegs, back to normal. Francis was overjoyed. She could probably take it better than he could – what a relief.

"This calls for a celebration. Where's Giles?"

"Oh, he's around somewhere, though I'm not particularly bothered one way or the other."

Serve him right if he loses her, thought Francis as he bought the drinks. He's been taking her for granted for ages – too conceited, that's his problem.

"Cheers." They clinked glasses, drank and kissed while their mouths were still wet. "Steady, sailor – you don't want to ruin my reputation do you?"

"What reputation?"

They got on so well together. She was such fun to be with. No regrets, no recriminations. How lucky he was to have met her.

"Where's Giles?" he asked again.

"Haven't seen him for ages – he doesn't seem to mind whether I'm here or not."

"Why on earth do you put up with him?"

"Because I'm daft, I suppose."

Bruno and Alfonso arrived the next morning with gloomy news.

"We've been called up," they said.

"You can't possibly be called up again – it's illogical."

"Yes we have – look here."

"These are recall papers – you had special leave of absence to come here and now they've caught up with you. Don't worry – you won't have to go until next week. Let's have a look – yes, you have to be back by midnight on Sunday week – and don't look so miserable, you've got another ten days yet."

"What's going to happen to my uncle?"

Alfonso was particularly upset.

"Don't worry, he's quite safe here – anyway, he'll be going home soon – he'll probably be out of here before you leave."

"I'd like a word with you in my office – when you've finished your conversation, that is."

"Sorry Staff, I was just reassuring Alfonso that his uncle will be safe in your capable hands."

"Never at a loss for words are you, Francis. You might like to know that the Administrator came to see me personally yesterday afternoon and said they'd decided to close this ward after all – typical, isn't it? Armies of workmen, painters, decorators, telephone engineers, awning constructors, etc., etc., toiling night and day for the past two weeks, not to mention highly skilled staff, taken on specially to help cope with hundreds of casualties – and what happens? – nothing. Anyhow, we've got another ten days or so to move the few remaining patients and close the ward, then I'm afraid we shall both be looking for other jobs – no, not other jobs altogether, but relocation within the hospital. They've already offered me a post in staff training and, as for you, I'm afraid you'll be back in Casualty."

Could be worse. He'd always had a feeling that the double promotion wouldn't last. He'd be much better off as a porter. Not so complicated.

"Don't forget that the ear consultant is coming this afternoon to sort out the final bed cases, including Alfonso's uncle. They're all more or less ready for discharge, so I expect Mr Cipriani will be able to go home on Sunday. I'll let him know for certain as soon as the consultant has finished."

The consultant had already arrived when they returned from lunch. He had an assistant with him and they were busy removing wax from Mr Cipriani's ears. There was an incredible amount of wax floating in the bowl. No wonder he hadn't been able to hear very well.

"Just look at this," said the consultant. "Both outer membranes intact – saved by sixty years of accumulated wax – never seen anything like it – just goes to show that nature provides its own protection if given a chance. This man is fine now – he can go home at any time."

"Immediately!" shouted Alfonso, beside himself with excitement.

"You must forgive him," said Staff. "This is Alfonso and Mr Cipriani is his uncle. He's been so worried about him."

"Well – he's as fit as a fiddle now."

The specialist shook Alfonso's hand and Staff followed him into the next ward.

"What's a fiddle?" asked Alfonso, apprehensively.

Bruno patiently translated, while Francis, feeling somewhat redundant, decided to do the washing up.

Alfonso, who had been busy on the telephone, joined him in the kitchen.

"My uncle has spoken to his relatives on the phone and they will come down on Sunday to collect him – they will hire a minibus."

"Good heavens," said Francis, "has he got all those relatives?"

"More," said Alfonso. "There is only room for ten and my uncle will need two of those seats, so only eight can come. There is considerable discussion among the family to decide who are the closest, for the privilege of bringing him home."

How lovely to have all those relatives, thought Francis. He'd only got a few himself and most of them would rather die than have to collect him from hospital. They'd probably draw lots to decide which of them would be the unlucky one to draw the short straw.

fourteen

"Don't take no notice of 'er – they'm all the same." Mr Curry coughed vigorously.

"I remember when I 'ad dysentery during the war – North Africa, it were. I were sick for days and they were always on at me. I 'ad some good times, mind you. I remember meeting me brother, unexpected-like. I were a driver, see, and we was driving through the desert when we saw another convoy coming straight at us. I pulled in a bit to let 'em pass and I suddenly seed me brother on top of a lorry – 'adn't seen 'im for ages, couldn't believe me eyes. I yelled out to 'im, but 'e never seed me, so I jammed on me brakes and waved and shouted at the top of me voice. Then he suddenly seed me and jumped down off the lorry and everything stopped – fifty bloody lorries in the middle of the desert, all stopped, just for us. I jumped out of me cab and ran to meet him and everyone thought us were mad, but I were so 'appy to see 'im I could 'ave cried. 'Adn't seen 'im since us left England, see – didn't know if 'e were alive or dead. 'Ell of a row, there was, but us didn't mind. They stuck us in the same bunch after that and us stayed together 'till the end of the war."

Francis thought of the millions of people who'd been caught up in the war. What a wonderful thing memory is, to be able to leave behind the sand, the flies and the decaying corpses and to remember, as if it were yesterday, the sheer joy of that incredible meeting.

Peggy was in the pub, but with Giles this time.

"Hello Frankie."

Giles frowned. "What's all this about 'Frankie'?"

"It's just that I prefer it to Francis – it's more masculine, somehow."

Steady girl, thought Francis, we don't want him to start thinking. Giles is no fool.

"Giles' mother has invited me to tea tomorrow afternoon, so I'm afraid we can't help you house-hunt after all. I'm so sorry."

News travels fast, he thought. Giles' mother must have heard about their visit last Sunday, not too much, hopefully, but just enough to make her wonder whether Peggy was a suitable companion for her son.

He waited until Giles went up to the bar before asking the million dollar question.

"Think she suspects anything?"

"Something, but not too much – at least, I hope not."

They grinned at each other, conspirators, somehow.

"The Italians seem quite popular," said Giles when he returned.

"It would be nice," said Francis, "if we could give them a good send-off next week-end before they return to their unit on Sunday – perhaps here. What do you think?"

"Good idea, I'll have a word with the landlord and see what he thinks. It will have to be a surprise, mind."

Trust Giles, ever the organiser.

He soon returned.

"The landlord thinks it would be a good idea. Saturday evening would be best. No, not tomorrow, you dope – Saturday week – the day before they leave. He's offered to present a cake on behalf of the regulars. They're a couple of nice lads and the regulars assume that they're a couple of army doctors on leave. I remember telling everyone last week, so the news must have spread."

"Isn't that a bit over the top? Suppose a real doctor came in?"

"Doctors are in and out all the time, but they don't mix much with the regulars – hospital hierarchy and all that."

Francis had a sudden thought.

"How about us and the other conchies who come here. Who do they think we are?"

" I told them we're medical students, which is true, up to a point."

Giles loved showing off. Perhaps he felt insecure. Whatever the problem, thought Francis, he's certainly a good organiser. He had already written Bruno and Alfonso's names on a piece of paper.

"I'll give it to the landlord, then he can write their names on top of the cake," he said.

"How about 'good luck' or 'thank you from all your friends'," suggested Francis.

"We don't want to get too sentimental," said Giles. "I think 'good luck' would be best. By the way, the landlord suggests sixpence each – that would be enough to buy a good cake and anything left over can go in the kitty."

They duly handed over their sixpences.

"Don't forget," said Francis, "tell the landlord it's got to be a complete surprise. I'll get them both here at eight o'clock exactly tomorrow week so that everyone who has contributed can be there to greet them."

"And a great many more, if I know anything about pubs," said Giles, "nothing like the prospect of a free drink to bring in the punters."

Francis and Peggy exchanged smiles – Giles, the quintessential cynic.

"Incidentally," said Francis, "you're not the only one to be invited out tomorrow,"

"Don't say you've got a date, Frankie?"

"No, not exactly – Bruno and Alfonso have invited me to dinner."

"Lucky you, I'd much rather go with you than have to spend a boring afternoon with Giles' mother."

"Never mind," whispered Francis. "At least you'll be able to find out just how much she knows."

"Hello, you're Francis, aren't you? I'm Mrs Oke, Bruno and Alfonso's landlady. Please come in."

What a nice lady, small and neat and very friendly and outgoing. There was a smell of cooking and the table in the front room was laid for four. Wouldn't be long now.

"I'm so hungry I could eat a horse," said Francis

"We don't eat horses in Italy," said Alfonso, worried as usual.

"Just a figure of speech," explained Bruno, patiently.

"Ah – I remember now," said Alfonso. "Just a figure of speech."

"Supper's ready. I hope you don't mind my joining you."

Mrs Oke brought in the supper and sat down.

It was a delightful meal and, after coffee, she produced a half bottle of cherry brandy. They sat round the table and talked. She told them about her husband, who had worked at the hospital and who had died recently.

They talked and talked and, the more Francis listened to Mrs Oke, the more he liked her.

"I shall miss the boys when they go," she said, "they're the first visitors I've had since Mr Oke died – the house will feel empty when they've gone."

Francis suddenly had an idea, a splendid idea if it worked out.

"Have you anyone in mind?" he asked.

"Not at the moment, but I expect something will crop up, sooner or later."

He would have to move quickly before it was too late.

"What a lovely home you've got." he said. "Could I possibly have a look around?"

"Of course." Mrs Oke was delighted.

They inspected the ground floor, two rooms downstairs and a large kitchen.

"I spend a lot of time in the kitchen – it's nice and warm in there. Mr Oke and I always sat there in the evenings. Would you like to see upstairs?"

One large bedroom with a nice double bed, a smaller bedroom and a bathroom.

Why hadn't he thought of it before? They'd been so keen to get a flat on their own that he hadn't even thought of possible alternatives. Joanna would be working all day and she'd welcome a meal when she came home. And he was sure they'd get on well together.

He heard Bruno and Alfonso downstairs. Alfonso had started to sing. The cherry brandy was doing its stuff. It was now or never.

"I hope you won't mind my asking," he said, "but would there be any possibility of my wife and I coming here for a few weeks? She's starting in the Almoner's office in two weeks' time and we haven't got anywhere to live at the moment."

Mrs Oke hesitated for a brief second.

"How about your wife?" she asked. "What does she think about it?"

"I don't know yet," said Francis, "but I'm sure you'd get on well together. I just know you would. What would you charge? And could we possibly have the double room upstairs?"

Mrs Oke hesitated again.

"I haven't used that room since Mr Oke died, but it can't stay empty for ever. Let's say it's yours for as long as you want it, and I charge two pounds ten each, including breakfast and evening meal, the same as the Italian boys – they've been using the front room downstairs."

Five pounds a week, including meals – quite a bargain.

"Thank you so much, Mrs Oke. I'm sure my wife will be delighted to come here. I'll phone her tomorrow and let you know tomorrow evening."

They went downstairs and helped themselves to the last of the the cherry brandy, then Francis thanked Mrs Oke for her hospitality and said goodbye to Bruno and Alfonso. Bruno was packing his suitcase.

"I'm going away for a few days," he said. "I'll be back by Thursday for Bill and Rosina's party and we'll both meet you in the pub on Saturday evening at eight o'clock."

"Guess what?" Alfonso seemed quite excited. "He's got a date – a nurse at the hospital – they're going to Blackpool together."

"Have a nice time Bruno," said Francis, "and don't do anything I wouldn't."

Bruno looked at him quizzically.

"It all depends," he said, "must go now – my train leaves at eight."

fifteen

With nothing much else to do, Francis sorted out his get-well cards. Anything to pass the time. Baby mice sitting up in bed, cute looking rabbits, mournful dogs with bandages round their noses, stupid looking birds with get well cards clamped in their ridiculous beaks – all unbelievably trite and all probably drawn by the same so-called artist. How dreadful they were – anyone capable of sending such atrocious cards couldn't possibly care whether he got well or not. It was a ritual, like Christmas. . .

'Better send one to Francis.' – 'Francis who?' – 'You know, Joanna's Francis.' – 'Oh, him. I didn't even know he was ill, what's wrong with him?' – 'Goodness only knows.' Goodness only cared, he thought – apart from his own immediately family.

"Mumbling to yourself again, I see."

Nurse Jarrett, back from Persia already.

"I dreamt about you last night, nurse. We flew away together on a magic carpet."

"Fancy that, now."

Just as he feared. The wretched girl was totally uninterested. He'd been hoping to bring the subject round to her breasts like water melons and her milky white thighs, but she was far too busy gawking at that new doctor with the runaway chin.

Chinless wonder came closer.

"Let's have a look at this man's back. Yes, I thought so – time his tube was changed."

"Certainly, doctor." She seemed quite excited.

"Fetch the trolley, will you."

"Certainly, doctor."

"No – not that trolley, nurse. Hurry up, please, I haven't got all day."

Chinless wonder prodded Francis between the shoulder blades, then he selected a thin plastic tube and inserted it into the wound. It didn't even hurt, but Francis winced convincingly.

"There, all done – you can put a dressing on now, nurse."

"Certainly, doctor."

She was still twittering, but her hands were smooth and gentle. Perhaps he'd tell her about his dream one day when he had a chance.

The Italian family had just arrived when Francis got to the hospital on Sunday. Mr James was trying to explain to the driver of a battered looking minibus that he couldn't park in front of the hospital.

"They've come to collect a patient," said Francis. "How about letting them go round the back to emergency – after all, they are a sort of ambulance."

"Funniest ambulance I've ever seen," said Mr James. "I suppose I could always look the other way and pretend I haven't seen them – all right, but be quick about it."

Francis signalled to the driver and led the way round the side of the hospital to the emergency entrance. He showed them where to park and they all piled out. They poured into the ward and embraced Mr Cipriani. The pandemonium increased as the children raced round the ward, shouting with excitement. It seemed to Francis that the whole event was more like an outing to Blackpool than a hospital visit.

"I only hope," said Staff, "that Sister doesn't arrive until they've gone. Just help me sort this lot out, will you? This is Nurse Collins, by the way – she comes in on Sundays so that I can have a bit of peace and quiet."

They had brought presents for everyone – flowers and chocolates for Staff, engraved cuff links for Francis – what on earth would he do with engraved cuff links? The children presented them with more flowers. Even Nurse Collins had a bouquet, and Mr Cipriani made a speech, in Italian, thanking them for all they had done for him. Bruno translated as best he could and they all stopped and listened.

Staff took the opportunity of thanking them in a loud voice before pandemonium broke out again.

"Thank you all," she said. "The ward will be closing in ten minutes and I'm sure Mr Cipriani would like to be on his way – you've got a long journey ahead of you." Bruno translated, and, with hugs and kisses, the invasion gradually subsided. Staff and Nurse Collins helped Mr Cipriani out to the minibus and settled him down in a large seat in the middle row, slightly raised above the others.

They stood round and clapped as he sat there. Looking through the window, the whole thing, in some strange way, reminded Francis of a Papal visit. The minibus, admittedly, lacked the splendour usually associated with a papal vehicle, but there was a certain similarity, which however was soon displaced as they all piled on board. How could so many people get into a minibus? And what would happen when it started? – if indeed it ever managed to start with such a load. The engine roared and the driver accelerated. They waved frantically and the papal vehicle gathered speed until it was out of sight.

They cleared up and Staff made a pot of tea, but Francis decided that something stronger was indicated. He called in at the pub on his way home for a beer and a sandwich. Peggy was there on her own, more desirable than ever.

"Do you always look as irresistible as this on Sundays?"

She accepted the compliment gracefully.

"How did you get on yesterday," he asked. "I hope Giles' mother hasn't heard of your promiscuity."

"Isn't that just like a man?" she observed. "How about you?"

"Why is it," asked Francis, "that women feel so threatened by the word 'promiscuous'?"

"Because we prefer not to be put down by people like you."

Good old Pegs – spirited – giving back as good as she got. Why on earth did she bother with Giles?

"Where's Giles?" he asked.

"With his wretched mother, I expect."

So, she had heard something – not too much, he hoped.

"I sat there for two hours yesterday while she quizzed me. How did I meet you? What was I doing with you last Sunday? Why wasn't Giles with us? Why wasn't your wife there? I could have screamed, and I very nearly did. Giles, the wretch, didn't back me up at all. He just sat there like a dumb cluck, looking uncomfortable. If I wanted to go out with a mummy's boy, I'd have chosen someone with a lot more money than he's got. He's constantly borrowing money from me and he never pays me back. And there's his wretched mother, sitting there like Lady Muck, daring to criticise me. I wouldn't mind so much if she had the guts to come out with it, but no – she's far too ladylike to call a spade a spade. People like her make me sick."

Quite a speech, really. Peggy looked magnificent when she was angry.

"How infuriating," said Francis. "I'm surprised you put up with it for so long."

"I don't know why I did, either. Perhaps I should have my head examined."

"Come on, Pegs, she's not worth bothering about – or that wretched son of hers. Let me get you something to drown your sorrows."

"Good old Frankie. You always manage to cheer me up."

He returned from the bar with a beer, a G&T and two spam sandwiches. They were usually pretty awful, but these were edible – just.

"Will you be seeing Giles again?"

"I don't know. I don't think so, but you never know."

"Must go now – cheers, Pegs – and keep your pecker up."

"Cheers, Frankie, and thanks for everything."

sixteen

"Wouldn't mind a couple of those to play with – beats me 'ow they manage to grow 'em so big."

Mr Curry, at it again, gloating over his playmate of the month.

"Let's have a look then."

Francis leaned over and took the magazine. He opened it and flicked over the pages until he came to the reclining beauty in the middle. Mr Curry was right, the water melons were exceptionally large.

"Good morning to you – what have we here?"

The voice was unmistakable, it could only be the parson.

Francis considered the various possibilities. We have here breasts like water melons and milky white thighs – we have here a poor, pathetic creature, drooling over his playmate of the month – we have here a highly intelligent fellow, trying desperately to survive – we have here a frightened atheist, almost inclined to 'see the light' in exchange for survival. *Yer pays yer money and yer takes yer choice.*

"It all depends on your point of view," he said finally. The parson had already moved on to his next question.

"Is there anything I can do for you?" he asked.

How about a nice, fat, juicy steak? Or, come to that, a nice, fat, juicy nurse? Both infinitely preferable to a pile of pious platitudes.

"No thanks," said Francis. "There's nothing I need at the moment."

"Surely there must be something?"

The parson sounded disappointed – another lost sheep, perhaps, unwilling to return to the fold. Francis dragged himself away from his playmate of the month and looked around.

"Yes please," he said. "I'd like to get out of this dreadful place alive."

The parson seemed lost for words at such an unusual request.

"I'm sure you will," he said, absent-mindedly. "I'm sure you will." But his voice lacked conviction and he quickly changed the subject.

"We're holding a service in the television lounge this morning," he said. "Would you like to join us?"

Francis nodded. Anything to relieve the monotony.

The parson smiled, mission accomplished.

"Good – see you in half an hour then. I'll ask sister to arrange for a porter to collect you and bring you back."

Francis read *Playboy* from cover to cover and was just giving playmate of the month a final leer when the porter arrived with a wheelchair. Nurse Jarrett helped him into the chair and tucked him in.

"You'd better leave that magazine with me," she said, "just in case you lose it."

Francis smiled as he handed it over.

"There's a lovely photo of you inside," he said, "centre page I think."

"Rosina and I would like to welcome you all to our monthly get-together. There are quite a few new faces here to-night and we would like to give a special welcome to our Italian friends, Bruno and Alfonso, who will be leaving in a few days to return to their unit, and to thank them for their help during the past few weeks."

Bill was in expansive mood.

"Rosina, as usual, has conjured up the magnificent spread which you see before you. How she manages to do this, month after month, despite the problems of rationing, I will leave to your imagination. Suffice it to say, our friends in Scotland seem to be rather better off than we are as far as rationing is concerned and, as her mother lives in Scotland, food parcels from her are always welcome.

The bottles of Italian wine on the table are here by courtesy of Mr Cipriani, Alfonso's uncle, whose family run a restaurant in London. Mr Cipriani was injured recently in an air raid and he was evacuated to our hospital during the red alert. Fortunately, his injuries were not serious and, when his relatives came to collect him, they brought with them a case of wine, the contents of which you see before you.

Please help yourselves – red or white – to get us off to a good start. Thanks for coming and we hope you will do justice to their unexpected and extremely generous gift and, just for to-night, forget all about British Restaurant food, spam sandwiches, dried milk and dried bananas and drink a toast to Mr Cipriani and to Rosina's mother for their kindness in contributing so much towards this evening's entertainment."

They all clapped and someone tried to thank Bill and Rosina, but no-one heard him – they were all too busy jostling for position at the feast. Francis poured himself a large glass of wine, took a slurp and topped his glass up again while the going was good.

"Steady on, old boy – you're not the only aspiring alcoholic here, you know."

It was Giles of course. Francis might have known that he wouldn't be far behind.

The chatter intensified.

"Where d'you think she managed to get all this?"

"Off the back of a lorry, perhaps."

"No, she wouldn't do a thing like that – don't forget they're Quakers. Didn't you hear what Bill said about her mother in Scotland?"

"Must have cost a fortune in postage – she must think we're all starving or something."

"Well, we are, aren't we?"

The feast disappeared in a remarkably short time and Francis looked around. All the familiar faces were there – even Ray, who was sitting on his own, but actually smiling.

"Glad you managed to come after all. Here, you'd better take these before they all go."

Rosina, ever perceptive, handed Ray the last plate of sandwiches and left him to it. Then she collared Bruno and Alfonso and gave them some sheet music of arias from Italian operas before dragging them over to the old upright piano in the corner of the room and striking a chord to command attention.

"Bruno and Alfonso are now going to sing for us – arias from some of their favourite operas. We're going to rehearse first, so carry on with your chitter-chatter until we're ready."

Bruno and Alfonso, sheepish at first, rapidly gained confidence. Bruno in particular had a magnificent bass voice, all the better for being so totally unexpected. The two sang well together, while Rosina played the piano and they all joined in the choruses.

Afterwards, while the others were doing the washing up, Francis, who, as usual, had succeeded in avoiding participation in menial tasks, wandered into the next room and found Bruno and Rosina, deep in conversation.

"Non-violent resistance to tyranny is a wonderful idea," Bruno was saying, "and I admire you for your beliefs, but it just doesn't work with bullies – you have to fight back. Hitler and Mussolini are trying to dominate the world. German bombers are destroying your towns and cities and their submarines are sinking hundreds of your ships each month, while our Russian friends are fighting for their lives. Millions of Russians have already died, defending Moscow, Stalingrad and Leningrad, while the Americans sit on the fence and wait to see who will win the war in Russia before they decide what to do about it."

"Are you a Communist?" asked Rosina, because. . ."

"Yes, I always have been," interrupted Bruno. "It's the only way to fight for a better world. I've volunteered to fly to Yugoslavia to join Tito and his partisans who are fighting the Germans in Serbia. They need all the help they can get and I'm learning to speak Serbo-Croat in the hope that your government will let me join one of the special medical units which fly out to North Africa and Yugoslavia each month."

"However will it all end?" asked Rosina.

"It will end when the Russians have defeated the Germans," said Bruno. "Maybe not straight away, but the end will be in sight then, thanks to Britain and Russia – but no thanks to America."

Francis was impressed – Bruno's idealism and that of millions like him was so strong that, not for the first time, he felt a sense of failure, maybe because he was doing so little to help win the war.

He left them to it and wandered round the room. Bill and Rosina hadn't been there long and chairs and tables were still stacked in a corner where the removal men had left them. And then he saw it – a lovely old gramophone, very similar to the one that had been his pride and joy all those years ago. There were some old records in the cupboard, including some with the magical black and gold labels which had so entranced him in the basement of his old home. He suddenly saw himself, riding round and round on his tricycle, stopping only to wind up the gramophone, and put on his favourite record – the one with the familiar labels, Rossini's *William Tell* on one side and Tchaikovsky's *1812* on the other.

Full of wonder, he lifted the heavy twelve inch records out of the cupboard and spread them out on a table, and there it was – the 1812 overture. He could hardly believe his eyes.

"Come and see," he shouted to Bruno. "This wonderful old record of Tchaikovsky's 1812 overture to celebrate Napoleon's retreat from Moscow, long before you were born."

Bruno and Rosina came over to look at the record and Rosina wound up the gramophone and put in a new needle.

"We bought this old gramophone at an auction a few months ago," she said. "I didn't even know about the records – let's see if it works."

And work it did, very slowly at first and then, with a helping hand, gathering speed while they wound the handle to keep it going. Bill gave it a squirt or two of oil to stop the squeaking and they all gathered round and listened, entranced, while the bells of Moscow rang out, the cannons roared, and Napoleon was well and truly vanquished.

"There, you see," said Bruno, "the Russians are a great people – first Napoleon and now Hitler. Why are you British so suspicious of the Russians?"

The party broke up at midnight and they staggered out into the road. Francis did his best to keep them in order, but they seemed to have no idea where they were going and insisted on singing Italian arias out of tune. Eventually, Bruno, like an old warhorse with a fine instinct for the way home, plodded in the right direction and Francis handed them over safely to Mrs Oke before going on his way, with the 1812 overture ringing in his ears.

seventeen

Staff was waiting for Francis when he arrived on Monday.

"Sister, from Casualty, has just been here and I agree with her that there's no point in flogging a dead horse."

"You mean me, Staff?"

"No, you clot, not you – the ward, this ward. I don't think you're dead quite yet."

She laughed, a throaty, infectious laugh, quite sexy really.

"I shall be having a well deserved break for the next fortnight and Nurse Collins will help you with the inventory. Our two remaining patients will be moved to a medical ward and someone from stores will be coming this afternoon to count the beds, tables and chairs. The clean linen will be returned to laundry and you will deal with the dirty linen – all of it – sheets, blankets, pillow cases, anything that looks used or crumpled, just bin it. Your nice new bin will come in handy after all."

"How about pillows, Staff, and cushions?"

"Trust you to think of something I haven't mentioned. Just take them to Casualty and leave them in the rest room. I'm sure they'll sort them out when they see them."

"How about you, Staff?"

"Oh, I expect my husband will sort me out when he sees me. How about you?"

"I thought, perhaps, a crafty week-end in the Cotswolds with a nice student nurse for company – or even a sexy staff nurse if all else fails."

"I thought you said your wife was coming to join you at the end of the week."

"Not this week, Staff – next week."

"Anyway, I think that's all for the moment. You should be finished here by tomorrow evening, so you'd better report to Casualty on Wednesday morning. You never know, you might even find yourself a nice student nurse to compensate for your monastic existence since you've been here."

Nurse Collins was a nice little thing, attractive, dark brown hair and a roguish smile.

They spent the morning stripping the beds and piling up a mountain of sheets and blankets for the bins. The laundry came to collect the clean linen and Francis took the pillows and cushions down to Casualty in his bin trolley. He sneaked into the rest room and piled them in a corner without being spotted, then he returned and sorted the rest into two piles – really dirty for binning and the rest for the laundry to collect at the end of the week. Why on earth they couldn't have collected it at the same time as the clean linen he would never know – perhaps it was something to do with cross infection. Then he loaded up the rest for Ray at lunchtime and set off through Casualty as usual.

"I might have known it was you – what's that pile of cushions and pillows doing in the rest room?"

"Staff told me to put them there."

"I have no recollection of telling you to do any such thing, Francis."

"No, I mean the other Staff – she's just gone off duty."

"Has she now. Surely your common sense should have told you that cushions and pillows should not be abandoned in our rest room without first checking that we wish to have them here?"

"I was just doing what I was told, Staff."

"Of course, although I don't recollect such admirable sentiments when you first came. Perhaps, when you start with us again on Wednesday, we shall reap the benefit of your change of heart."

Good old Staff, although he'd have to remember to be less outspoken with this one. And how on earth did she know that he was returning to Casualty on

Wednesday? Everyone seemed to know what he was doing long before he knew it himself. That, he realised, was something he would have to get used to – being bottom of the pile.

"Francis, Sister wants to see you in her office."

He couldn't believe it. He'd only just arrived and already trouble was looming. What on earth was wrong now? He suddenly remembered the pillows and cushions in the rest room. Surely they weren't still there?

"Ah, Francis, I feel I owe you an explanation. You remember coming to my office a few weeks ago when the Italians arrived. I assumed – wrongly, as it turned out – that you were a qualified ward orderly, sent to work with them for a few days to smooth out any language and other difficulties which might arise. With the benefit of hindsight, I should of course have checked your qualifications before asking you to work with them. Please accept my apologies. You may go now."

So the whole thing was a mistake – the ward orderly that never was. He'd be the laughing stock of the ward if he wasn't careful.

"Thank you for explaining, Sister. I did wonder what it was all about."

Staff was lurking outside the door.

"Why didn't you tell me?" he asked. "I hope no one else knows besides you."

"I'm sorry, Francis, I really am. No one else knows and I'll make sure that no one does – as long as you do as you're told. Just remember that I know what happened."

Francis took a chance.

"Did you enjoy your holiday in Blackpool?" he asked, casually.

She blushed. Staff actually blushed. "I don't know what you're talking about," she said crossly. But he knew that the gamble had paid off – it was true.

"You probably know that the Italians will be leaving on Sunday, but you may not know that we're giving them a farewell party on Saturday evening – 8 pm at the pub.

All their friends will be there and we've contributed towards a special farewell cake. They don't know about it yet, but we'll make sure that they're there by eight o'clock. If you should see Bruno before then, don't say anything to him about it. It's going to be a great send off and a real surprise."

Francis realised, too late, that the hymn had finished and everyone was sitting down except him. Perhaps he could rush forward and pretend to be saved, but he decided that the television lounge was hardly the place for histrionics and he couldn't rush far anyway, so he sat down sheepishly. Salvation would have to wait. The parson was rambling on and on, something about forgiving your enemies. Francis listened for a while, remembering a time during the war when he might have agreed, but the church militant had preached a different doctrine then, blessing the colours and encouraging people to kill one another. Then, when it was all over, they had the cheek to start preaching forgiveness all over again.

"And so, my friends, forgiveness is Christ's weapon against his adversaries."

Tell that to the marines. But the sermon was ending now and his back was aching terribly. All he wanted now was to get back to the ward and lie down.

"So glad you could come. Don't forget that we meet here again on Friday morning."

Over my dead body, thought Francis, which it probably would be if he didn't hurry up and get back into bed. Serve him right, he should have stayed where he was instead of crawling to the Almighty just because he was afraid of dying.

Francis met Giles while he was waiting in X-ray. He hadn't seen him since his brief encounter with Peggy a few days before.

"Come and have a cup of tea," said Giles, "your patient won't be ready for half an hour at least – she's right at the end of the queue. By the way, have you seen Peggy recently?"

He seemed casual enough, though you could never be sure with Giles.

"Yes, I saw her in the pub Sunday lunchtime. She seemed to be a bit fed up with you."

"Hardly surprising, really. My mother was particularly obnoxious when she came to tea on Saturday. I didn't know what to say."

Quite an admission, coming from Giles, although it made sense. Francis suddenly felt sorry for him – with a mother like that, it was hardly surprising that he had felt unable to intervene. Dominant mothers, he thought, had a lot to answer for when it came to letting go of their sons.

"Cheer up, old chap, why don't you give her a nice box of chocolates and say how sorry you are that you didn't stick up for her last week."

Giles hesitated, the thought of actually apologising had obviously never occurred to him.

"D'you really think I should do that?"

"Of course. Haven't you ever apologised to anyone before?"

Giles didn't answer.

"Tell you what," said Francis, "next Saturday, when we meet at the pub to say goodbye to Bruno and Alfonso, why not invite Peggy? She couldn't possibly say no to that, then you can present her with the chocolates and ask to be forgiven – on bended knee if necessary."

Giles smiled for the first time. "That'll be the day," he said, "but thanks for the good, fatherly advice. You should have been a psychologist."

Francis wheeled his patient back to Casualty. How nice to feel that Giles and Peggy would be reunited, then they could all go out together to celebrate Joanna's arrival at the end of next week

He felt quite exhausted by lunchtime on Saturday. The new staff nurse in Casualty certainly kept him at it and his feet were aching something shocking as he limped down to the pub.

Giles and Peggy – together again already – splendid.

"Whatever's wrong with you?" asked Giles. "You look like death warmed up."

"Unlike you," said Francis, "I've been putting in some overtime."

"Whatever for?" asked Giles. "I thought overtime went out with the Ark."

You've obviously forgotten there's a war on," said Francis. "Some of us are doing our best to pull our weight.

"Listen to who's talking," said Giles.

"Stop it, you two – stop quarrelling and buy me another gin."

The spam sandwiches were more than usually revolting, so Francis bought three more gins to take the taste away and took the opportunity of checking with the landlord.

"All set for to-night?"

"Yes, everything ready. The cake's a beauty and we've got enough left over for two lots of drinks all round."

Just as well, thought Francis, he'd spent far too much on booze this week. He'd have to start economising from now on. But it would certainly help when Joanna arrived and they had somewhere nice to live instead of his grotty boarding house.

They left the pub together and he was pleased to see Giles and Peggy holding hands as they walked.

More visits to X-ray, but different this time. They poured a thick white fluid down his tube. Francis watched it go down on the television monitor and he wondered what would happen when it reached his lung.

"Don't worry, it's fully absorbent – we need to show up your abscess on the X-ray."

So he had an abscess, had he? He could hardly wait to get back to the ward.

"Anyone got a dictionary?"

'Abscess – a localised collection of pus, formed in the body by disintegration of the tissue.' So he was disintegrating, was he? – with pus in his lung. How the hell did it get there? – and was it getting better or worse?

He felt like one of Major Peel's rats, caught in a trap from which there was no escape. He'd always assumed that he would recover eventually, but now he was really frightened. Why on earth didn't they tell him the truth?

He hadn't long to wait. The great man himself – and at teatime, too.

"Hand me those X-rays, will you? Hmm – don't think much of this lot."

The vultures were gathering for the kill – Mr Nandi, Chinless Wonder, Fisheye, even his beautiful Indian doctor – all there, waiting to pronounce the Sentence of Death. The great man glared at his X-rays.

"These are completely useless – see that they're done again." He turned to Francis. "We'll have to keep you in for another few weeks."

It took a while for the words to sink in. He was going to live after all. A few casual words and he was actually going to live. All his fears and anxieties suddenly exploded. They were all so bloody casual – the gallows had gone and they hadn't even noticed. He wanted to cry out and thank them, but they weren't even looking.

Francis fought back the tears and tried to concentrate. Words were so terribly important. How essential it was to be able to understand them properly.

'We'll have to keep you in for another few weeks' – ten little words and you were free. 'To be hanged by the neck until you are dead' – ten little words and you were dead, just like that. They leave you alone with your fears, they never say anything, they never answer your questions, until one day, out of the blue, quite casually, you're either free or you're dead.

His rage evaporated as quickly as it had come and he was overcome with relief and gratitude. He was going to live. They could do anything they liked to him now – anything. The hot sun streamed through the window and he dabbed his eyes with a handkerchief, but the tears were still there, blurring his vision. He lay back on his pillow, exhausted, and looked around as though for the first time. The bright colours of the flowers blurred into an impressionist painting, full of ripples and reflections. It was good not to have to worry, to lay there quietly, soaking up the sun, the colours and the blurred images, content just to be alive.

eighteen

The pub was quite full when Francis arrived that evening. News had obviously got around that there was something happening and, as Giles had so accurately foretold, the hangers on, hopeful for a free drink, were already there, together with several nurses. Alfonso had obviously had some success, he thought as he surveyed the local talent, and then, sitting together at a table, well away from the nurses, were his very own staff nurses – the Blackpool Belle from Casualty and his favourite from the Nissen huts. How very nice to see them there.

They were laughing at something, then they looked up and saw Francis and tried not to laugh. So, they were talking about him, were they? And laughing at the same time. He knew exactly why they were laughing – the ward orderly that never was. Now was the time to play his ace, all the more effective for being unexpected. He walked up to their table.

"Good evening", he said, "so glad you could come." Then, turning to the Blackpool Belle, "I hope you enjoyed your holiday – how was Blackpool?"

"I quite enjoyed it," she said, cool as a cucumber. "It made a nice change."

He had to hand it to her, she didn't blink an eyelid.

"You never told me you went to Blackpool," said her friend.

"No, it seemed a funny place to go for a day trip, but I'd never been there before so I thought I'd give it a try."

She looked so beseechingly at Francis that he just had to let her off the hook.

"Can I get you two ladies a drink?" he asked, gallantly.

"That's very kind of you, Francis." She looked at her friend. "Gin and tonics would be very welcome."

It was only on his way to the bar that he remembered that he'd been buying gin and tonics – mostly for other people – all day. His last pound note had gone and he only had a few bob in his pocket. He leaned over the bar.

"Could you possibly lend me a pound?" he whispered to the landlord.

The landlord hesitated.

"I don't normally lend money," he whispered, "but seeing it's you I'll make an exception. Don't tell anyone for goodness sake, otherwise every scrounger in the hospital will be after me for loans and I'll be out of business in no time. You medical students are the worst."

He took a pound out of the till and passed it to Francis.

"Thanks very much," said Francis, "I'd like three gin & tonics."

"Have those on the house," said the landlord.

Francis smiled gratefully. Not only a pound, but three gin & tonics as well – it must be his lucky day

"Here you are ladies," he said. "I think it's about time you told me your names – it gets a bit boring calling you both 'Staff' all the time. I promise not to divulge your names or other incriminating information whilst on duty."

They looked at one another.

"I'm Bridget," said Casualty Staff.

Bridget the Blackpool Belle, thought Francis. Pity he'd promised not to divulge anything – a great title like that could have been all round the hospital in no time.

"And I'm Lesley," said Nissen Staff.

That's better, he thought – an attractive name for an attractive woman.

They drank up and he left them to it. It was nearly eight o'clock and he wanted to join Giles and Peggy for the great moment. And a great moment it was too – better than anyone could have imagined. The door opened and there they were – Bruno and Alfonso, resplendent in military uniforms. They marched up to the bar and there was a round of applause as they gave the landlord a full military salute.

"Drinks all round," said Bruno in a clipped, upper class accent.

Goodness knows where he got it from. Perhaps he was specially coached by the Blackpool Belle while they were resting from their labours, but, however achieved, it was certainly impressive.

There was instant pandemonium as everyone crowded to the bar to take full advantage of the generous offer – and from army doctors as well. Giles had told the regulars that they were army doctors, but they had only half believed him, and now they could see for themselves. Bruno and Alfonso were their good friends, who had come to help out during the recent emergency and were now returning to their units. It was up to them, the regulars, to give them a good send off.

The landlord suddenly remembered the cake, which he produced like a rabbit out of a hat. "Quiet everyone," he shouted in a commanding voice. He hadn't been a landlord for twenty years for nothing. Silence reigned as he presented the cake to Bruno and Alfonso with a flourish.

"We're sorry you're leaving," he said, "but we hope you'll come back and see us again after the war."

A cheer went up, but he hadn't finished yet.

"To mark the occasion," he shouted above the din, "we've still got money in the kitty, so it'll be drinks all round until it's empty."

More cheers and cries of 'speech'.

Bruno had been half expecting to make a speech – it had been well rehearsed.

"On behalf of Alfonso and myself," he said in the same clipped, upper class voice, "I'd like to thank you all for this magnificent send off, which we will always remember. We certainly hope to come back and see you all again when the war is over."

"Long live Italy," shouted Alfonso.

A cheer went up at what might have been considered a somewhat inappropriate toast, but the regulars had been used to hearing him singing the Italian national anthem at closing time and they were far too busy gulping down their free drinks to worry about such minor details.

Francis looked around for Giles and Peggy, but the crush was so great that it was only when he heard Peggy's high pitched squeal that he was able to find her, on the floor, surrounded by ardent admirers. No Giles of course, he was never there when he was needed.

"Thank goodness you're here," she gasped. "I don't mind a mild flirtation, but this is the limit."

He extracted her from the mêlée and shunted her to the far corner of the pub. She should be safe there for a while.

"Hardly surprising you're so popular," he said, "in a dress like that."

"What's wrong with my dress?" she asked. As if she didn't know.

"It's devastating," he said. "It gives men ideas."

"I wish it would give Giles ideas," she said petulantly.

So that's what was wrong, he thought, and there wasn't anything he could do about it.

The pandemonium increased until the kitty was empty, then it gradually subsided as the free drinks ran out and the hangers-on departed, leaving the regulars to drink up and clear up. They found Giles behind the bar, drunk as a lord. Peggy cradled him in her arms and the landlord splashed some cold water in his face.

"Let 'im be," he said, "he'll soon be all right – nothing to worry about."

The Italian national anthem drew to a close and the regulars knew it was time to go. Bruno embraced everyone in sight, with a special embrace for the Blackpool Belle – only Francis and Lesley saw the tears in her eyes as he kissed her. "I must go now," he said softly, before turning to shake hands with the landlord, who seemed quite relieved not to be embraced. Alfonso was swaying from side to side and Bruno just managed to catch him before he collapsed.

"I've managed to get two taxis," said the landlord. "Quite an achievement on a Saturday night, what with petrol rationing and all. They'll be here in a few minutes."

They dragged Giles out from behind the bar and helped him to his feet. Peggy put her arm round him and walked him to the door.

She bundled him into the taxi, then she turned and gave Francis a very special kiss.

"Good night, Frankie dear," she said, "and thank you so much for everything."

Francis saw them off. A final embrace from Bruno, then he went inside to thank the landlord.

"We've had a wonderful evening," he said. "Thank you so much for all you've done – and I won't forget the pound I owe you."

"Forget it," said the landlord. "I enjoyed it too. They deserved a good send off. They're a couple of good lads and I wish them well."

Francis walked back to his digs. How nice people were when you got to know them. He felt somehow that he'd reached a turning point in his life. Joanna was arriving in a few days and they'd start a new life together. She'd never been much of a one for pubs, but he didn't mind – pubs were only too often a substitute for homes. They would have a home together now for the first time and he could concentrate on the things that really mattered, Joanna and the work he was doing. Hospital work, however dreary, was his own choice – a choice infinitely better and more rewarding than the dreadful alternative of having to kill people. It was up to him now to prove that he could work really hard to help save life to justify his refusal to join in the killing.

Francis felt safe, warm and secure. The wonderful feeling of security reminded him somehow of his very first holiday by the sea, waking up to the smell of fried bacon, listening to his cousins laughing and talking in the next room, scraping their chairs on the wooden floor. Even now, fifty years on, he could still smell the bacon and hear their lively chatter as they sat down for breakfast, quite different from meals at home, with its snowy white tablecloth and silver teapot – everything formal, tense and silent. That's how he remembered it, so that was probably how it was.

Parents, he thought, have a lot to answer for, although they too were products of their own childhood. Perhaps part of the answer was to have several children. No one could be all that snobby with a mob of children rushing around. Even his mother's headaches might have disappeared if she had had something to do all day instead of just ringing for the maid to bring in the meals and clear the table. And yet, by all accounts, she had been a lively and attractive girl, vivacious, artistic and full of fun. So what had happened to change her? What had gone wrong? Perhaps she really had been ill and really had suffered from those dreadful headaches. The realisation of how ill she might have been made him feel ashamed. And yet, she had crippled his early life as surely as if he had been dropped from his pram.

"Cheerio, mate – I'm off now."

Francis was surprised to see that Mr Curry had dressed and was packing his bag.

"Surely you're not going home already?" he asked.

"Right first time, mate. I've 'ad enough of this bleeding place. I'm going 'ome 'afore they kill me."

"You'd better watch out," said Francis, "they'll stop you if you're not careful."

"Look 'ere, mate, there's nothing to stop me walking out of this bleeding place anytime I want."

Francis was impressed. It had never occurred to him that people could actually discharge themselves, just like that.

"How about your tube?" he asked.

"Sod the bleeding tube."

"But you can't just. . . "

"Watch me – got the wife waiting outside – quick get-away, see?"

He winked at Francis and picked up his bag.

"So long, mate. Take my advice and do the same before they finish you off."

Mr Curry strode down the ward, large as life, and no one tried to stop him. Then, with a final gesture of defiance, he pushed open the swing doors and was gone, taking his Playboy magazine with him. He had made his bed with military precision and his hospital dressing gown, neatly folded, was all that remained.

"What's happened to Mr Curry?"

"He's left, nurse – gone home – said he'd had enough of this bleeding place."

"No need to swear at me. You're quite sure he said he was going home?

"Yes, he said he'd had enough of this. . . "

"That's quite enough, Francis. It's not funny. Do try to behave yourself."

Mr Curry's sudden departure in defiance of hospital rules cheered him up no end. It needed guts, of course, to discharge yourself and he wasn't at all sure that it was a wise thing to do, but it was reassuring to know that it could be done. It made him feel less of a prisoner.

nineteen

The library trolley trundled down the ward and Francis asked the respectable lady in charge if she had a copy of *Playboy*.

"I'm afraid not. We don't encourage that sort of magazine here."

"What sort of magazine is it?" he asked, but she refused to be drawn.

"You'd sell a lot of copies," he offered, encouragingly, but she sniffed and carried on her way, her legs close together, registering their disapproval.

A sudden twinge reminded Francis that his back was still aching – worse, in fact, than it had been before they'd changed his dressing a few days ago. Time he made a fuss again. No one would bother otherwise.

"Yes, it does look a bit red. I'll ask Sister to have a look at it."

Sister wrinkled her nose in disapproval. "Would you take a look at this, doctor?"

Chinless Wonder prodded the incision.

"Let's have a look at his X-rays." He shuffled through the pack and held up the ace of spades, peering at it uncertainly, tutting and frowning

"This won't do at all. We'll have to put a new tube in."

"But doctor, you said I could go home next week."

"Well, I'm afraid you can't – not until we've cleared this lot up."

Caught again, a rat in a trap. He should have escaped with Mr Curry while he still had a chance. The pus was obviously still there, bottled up in his lungs, and he'd have to stay now, whether he liked it or not.

His X-rays lay on the bed where Chinless Wonder had left them. They stared at Francis and he glared back. They reminded him of huge, black crows, waiting to strike.

"Why are you looking at your X-rays?"

"I'm not looking at them nurse, they're looking at me. In any case, they're my X-rays."

"No they're not, they belong to the hospital."

His X-rays, the property of the hospital? Surely not. His bones, his ribs and his lungs in exchange for his life – and no guarantee even of that. The more he thought about it, the more one-sided it seemed. Even Faust did better than that, *he* would have had his pick of the nurses every night – and even Nurse Jarrett would have swooned in his arms, demanding to be ravished.

"What are you mumbling about now?"

"Only talking to myself, Sister."

"You really must try to calm down and not worry so much. You'll never get better if you carry on like this all the time."

She wasn't so bad, really. Quite nice in fact, but, as usual, far too busy to stay and talk. That's what he missed more than anything – someone to talk to – anything to take his mind off those damned crows.

Francis turned over on to his side, pressing his shoulder blades together to ease the pain. The crows were still there, dozens of them, gathering for the kill, massing at the foot of his bed. They were waiting to pounce as soon as he fell asleep, waiting to peck at his wound, waiting to tear his flesh away in huge, raw strips.

KILLER CROWS ATTACK PATIENT – HOSPITAL AUTHORITIES SUED FOR NEGLIGENCE

The headlines merged and the killer crows were there, smothering the patients, sucking their blood, repulsing all attempts to remove them by pecking wildly at anyone who came near them. The carnage continued until volunteers arrived with scalpels and put paid to the invasion by decapitating the crows until the survivors fled.

SILENT PROTEST – EXPERTS DIVIDED.

Members of the *Royal Society for the Protection of Birds* stood in silent protest outside the hospital gates yesterday, while an eminent ornithologist described the decapitations as disgraceful. Expert opinion is divided between those who maintain that the hospital had no choice but to take drastic action and those who consider that de-beaking would have sufficed.

Francis awoke in panic as the injection found his shoulder muscle and it was some time before he realised that the crows had really gone and he was still alive.

"Over you go."

"But I thought. . . "

"For goodness sake, stop talking and do as you're told."

He turned over on to his stomach and a pneumatic drill bored into his back between the shoulder blades. It was all over in ten seconds, but he went on yelling for some while. How dare they drill holes in his back without permission. He could sue them for damages.

"Do shut up, for heaven's sake. It's all over now – just lay still and keep quiet for a change."

He lay quite still as the new tube was inserted.

"Right, there we are. Put a dressing on and try to keep him quiet."

The pain had eased now and he lay there, pretending to be asleep.

"I see they've reduced you to silence." The familiar ecclesiastical voice again, the last thing he wanted at that particular moment.

"This god of yours," said Francis, "I've nothing in particular against him, but organised religion makes me sick."

"Sorry about that," said the voice. "We'll have to see what we can do about it, won't we?"

Patronising wretch, who the hell did he think he was? It seemed to Francis that he'd spent most of his life battling against authority – parents, teachers, headmasters, parsons, petty officials – the list was endless. And where had it got him?

"Penny for your thoughts."

"I was just thinking of you, nurse – how pretty you are."

Nurse Jarrett accepted the compliment with a smile.

"You've changed, nurse. You're much kinder now than you used to be."

"I know, I'm always nicer to people when they stop pinching my bottom."

"Who on earth would do a rotten thing like that?"

She looked at him, quizzically. "I wonder," she said.

"Looking better, I see." The parson was still there, interrupting their conversation, Adams apple working overtime.

Francis decided it was time to teach him a lesson.

"Have you ever pinched anyone's bottom?" he asked.

The apple paused in mid swallow and Nurse Jarrett beat a hasty retreat.

"I've sometimes thought about it, I must confess, but I've never actually done it."

Bully for him, the man was human after all.

"Why not?" asked Francis, but the parson was not to be drawn.

"I came to tell you about our Easter Service," he said.

Francis hesitated.

"Nurse Jarrett will be there."

That settled it – the man was worth supporting.

"In the television lounge then, eleven o'clock on Sunday."

twenty

"Jesus Christ is risen to-day."

Francis sang vigorously, the words coming easily from his childhood. This was his favourite hymn and he remembered asking his mother why it was only sung at Easter, simply to be told that it would not be appropriate to sing it at any other time. Why on earth, he thought, should we limit a good tune to Easter, just because the Church wanted to have everything their own way? Of course, if people were allowed to do things and enjoy their own god in their own way, what would become of the churches? People sang whatever hymns they liked in the Middle Ages. Surely the joy of singing was the important thing without churches setting themselves up as arbiters of what should be sung – and when.

The television lounge was packed. Even Sister was there, her shrill soprano voice only slightly off key. She was enjoying herself and her huge bosom heaved with Hallelujas. The pianist did his best, but even he sometimes wilted under the onslaught of her magnificent voice. The service was a great success and almost made up for the misery of Good Friday. Francis had always hated Good Fridays. The Crucifixion had been his very first introduction to deliberate cruelty – a cruelty so dreadful that it had given him nightmares for years. Even now, he could close his eyes and the horror would return, the rows of skulls, the nails hammered through flesh and bone, skewering men to the cross. Life was horrible enough without having to face up to such obscene brutality before you were ready for it. Then, whether you believed in Jesus or not, you were well and truly hooked on misery for one particular day each year conditioned like Pavlov's dogs to be miserable on Good Friday and happy again on Easter Sunday.

Whatever the reason, Francis felt much better on Easter Monday. He awoke in rare good spirits, yaffled up his breakfast and set out to explore the ward. His back still ached abominably, but he'd been living with it for several weeks now and a good night's sleep had worked wonders.

He shuffled gaily down the ward, smiling benevolently at his fellow patients and engaging them in conversation. His feeling of omnipotence grew with each step. "Yes – only a matter of time – wouldn't be surprised if they let you get up tomorrow; no – don't take any notice of her, she's always saying things like that; yes, that's typical – take my advice and tell her what you think of her."

"And what, may I ask, is that?"

"Nothing, Sister. I was just asking if there was anything I could do to help."

"I'm glad you're feeling so energetic. You can start with the tea trolley if you like."

Caught fair and square, his first morning up, too.

"I don't really feel strong enough to lift the big teapot, Sister. My back's aching and lifting the teapot might make it worse."

"Never mind, a little exercise will probably do it the world of good. And don't forget the empty cups."

Sweated labour, that's what it was. The headlines took shape as he collected the empties.

SLAVE LABOUR IN HOSPITAL – CRITICALLY ILL PATIENTS FORCED TO DO MENIAL TASKS – ALLEGATIONS OF CRUELTY DENIED

"What are you doing now?"

"Just thinking, Sister."

"Well go and think somewhere else will you. Some of us have work to do."

Francis decided to include the private patients in his errands of mercy. The private wing, as it was somewhat euphemistically called, consisted of three small rooms at the end of the corridor. These were technically out of bounds to ordinary patients, but Francis had never understood why – surely private patients, who were all on their own, should be allowed to mix with ordinary patients if they so wished. He waited until the coast was clear, then shuffled up the corridor. The first private room he came to was marked 'Mr Trent' and Francis rapped tunefully on the door.

"Come in."

He opened the door and introduced himself.

"Glad to meet you, old boy. Come in and take a seat. Bloody boring, stuck here all day with nothing to do."

"Glad I'm not intruding," said Francis.

"On the contrary – haven't seen a soul all day."

So far, so good, he was obviously welcome. Francis was just congratulating himself on his initiative when the door opened and Sister came in. She must have seen him after all.

"Just visiting, Sister."

"So I see. It's nearly lunchtime now, so perhaps you'd better go back to the ward." Francis, who had only just sat down, got up again and took leave of his new found friend.

"Come again, old boy – any time."

Francis grinned triumphantly at Sister.

"Of course I'll come again. I'm sure Sister won't mind."

He closed the door behind him and strode back to the main ward, almost forgetting to shuffle.

He kept out of Sister's way until Staff arrived. She seemed quite pleased when he offered to take tea to the private patients. Help from any quarter, however unexpected, was always welcome.

"I'll do Mr Trent first," he said. "I went to see him this morning and he's probably waiting to see me again,"

Secure in the knowledge that he was on official business, Francis hunted around in the kitchen – tea, bread and butter, and fruitcake which had definitely seen better days – and he was off up the corridor with Mr Trent's tray.

"Jolly decent of you, old boy."

Mr Trent reached under his bed and produced a bottle of whisky.

"Hate drinking on my own," he said.

Francis hesitated, then sat down and poured out Mr Trent's tea, while Mr Trent sloshed the whisky into two glasses and handed one to Francis.

"Cheers, old boy."

Francis grinned. Being a private patient certainly had its advantages.

"Same again, old boy?" But Francis was already on his feet.

"No thanks – really must go now, but thanks again."

Afternoon tea with Mr Trent was certainly going to be an interesting experience.

Back to the kitchen for the next tray – tea, bread and butter and more stale fruit cake.

"That's for number two – Mr Al-Rasheed – don't worry about the last room, there's no one there at the moment."

Francis knocked on the second door.

"Kom-een." Talk about doubtful ancestry, but friendly enough and obviously stinking rich. Thin, dark fingers clutched at the fruit cake, and beady eyes watched Francis intently while he poured out the tea. He didn't say anything and his fixed expression made Francis feel uncomfortable, almost as though Mr Al-Rasheed was a hawk waiting to pounce. He left as soon as he could and, as he had already forgotten his name, decided to call him him Hawkeye.

There was no name on the third door, but Francis took a look inside, just in case. The room was in darkness, so he switched on the light and was quite surprised to see someone lying on the bed.

"Thank goodness you've come."

A little man in pyjamas sat up in bed like a startled rabbit and gazed at him wildly. He seemed frightened and agitated and Francis wondered why he had been lying there in the dark – perhaps private patients had to pay for their own electricity. He thought of the lovely, large windows in the main ward and marvelled again at the thought of private patients actually paying to be shut up on their own when they could have been ordinary patients for nothing. Perhaps they had special privileges, perhaps they were allowed to indulge in some slap and tickle with the night staff or something like that, although, if appearances were anything to go by, the little man hardly seemed up to it. He looked so frightened and miserable that Francis decided to stay and keep him company for a while.

"I think they've forgotten me," said the little man. "I came in this morning and they told me to wait in here. I've been here ever since."

Francis, who had never believed in doing what he was told for any length of time, was amazed at such obedience.

"They said my bed wasn't ready yet and they told me to get undressed and wait here. Then someone came and took my clothes away and I've been on my own all day. I haven't had anything to eat, either."

"Don't worry," said Francis, "I'll get some tea and bread and butter and fruit cake for you if you like."

The little man grabbed the tray as soon as Francis returned and gobbled up the bread and butter as though his life depended on it. He even finished off the fruit cake, so he must have been pretty desperate.

Francis poured him another cup of tea.

"I was just wondering," Francis said, "why you didn't come out and ask someone?"

"I don't know, really – I don't have a dressing gown and I didn't like to. . ." He trailed off, miserably, and Francis began to understand what had happened. The little man, frightened out of his wits, doing exactly as he was told, too shy to come out without his dressing gown, too scared to bang on the wall. Yes, the only possible explanation was that he had been completely forgotten. No name on the door, no notes on the bed, no name tab on his wrist – in fact, no identity at all. The man who never was. Lucky the room had a toilet.

The whole thing was so preposterous that Francis couldn't help laughing to himself.

"Don't worry," he said, trying hard not to splutter, "I'll see what I can do."

He picked up the empty tray and opened the door.

"Don't worry," he said again, then he shut the door behind him and hooted with laughter. The Prisoner of Zenda, starving to death in a room the size of a broom cupboard. It really was too funny for words. He took the tray back to the kitchen and even began to wash up before he realised what he was doing.

twenty-one

The supper trolley was already parked in the corridor when Francis got back to the ward and the nurses were sorting out the diets.

Staff looked at her notes. "Anyone seen Mr Roberts? He should have come in this morning – there's a special diabetic diet for him – what shall I do with it?"

"Give it to the cat, by the look of it. Or, better still, give it to the little man in. . . "

Francis almost choked – the Prisoner of Zenda *was* Mr Roberts – and he, Francis, had just given him bread and butter, and fruit cake, and sugar in his tea! There was no time to lose, but Francis's cautious side told him to make absolutely sure before he said anything – wouldn't do to make a fool of himself. He slunk up the corridor, but the laundry had just been delivered and the door was blocked. Mr Roberts was trapped by a pile of laundry baskets and there was nothing that he, Francis, could do to rescue him. He'd have to tell Staff, and quickly.

"Staff, can I have a word with you?"

She looked at him suspiciously. They all stopped eating and listened expectantly.

"It's about Mr Roberts," said Francis. "Did you say he was diabetic?"

"He is, actually, but I don't see what that has to do with you. In any case, he doesn't seem to be here, does he?"

Francis gazed helplessly at the empty bed opposite and summoned up his courage. "It's Mr Roberts, Staff. I think he's in one of the private wards, the little one on the end. I didn't realise he was diabetic, so I gave him some bread and butter, and fruit cake. Oh. . . and sugar in his tea."

He realised as he spoke that he was becoming increasingly incoherent and Staff looked around, despairingly. Whatever next?

"He doesn't have a dressing gown," stammered Francis, " and the passage is full of laundry baskets. . . and he can't get out. He may starve to death if he's not rescued soon." It all sounded slightly absurd and Francis began to wonder if he was dreaming.

Staff was obviously of the same opinion. She walked slowly down the ward towards the corridor leading to the private wing. Francis was quite mad of course, it couldn't possibly be true. Or could it? She'd better go and make sure, just in case.

She was away for some time and there was a buzz of anticipation.

"Now you've done it. She'll get you for this."

Such excitement hadn't been equalled since Nurse Barker first arrived. She was amply endowed and her breasts contrived to strain outwards and upwards in defiance of the laws of gravity. There had been conflicting theories on the ward as to how she managed this and her arrival each morning was awaited with eager anticipation.

So it was with Staff, whose arrival – for very different reasons – was now eagerly awaited. Most of the patients knew by now that Francis was unpredictable, but was he totally mad? Was he really stupid enough to make the whole thing up?

They hadn't long to wait.

Staff returned with a grave face. "Nurse, ring for a porter, will you? Mr Roberts has arrived."

Staff went out of her way to be nice to Francis after that.

He was allowed to visit Mr Trent in the private wing each afternoon and they both looked forward to his visits. Mr Trent had acquired his own teapot and a supply of tea bags, and there was of course, always the whisky.

"Good for morale, old chap – next best thing to champagne."

They both knew the routine, tea first, then whisky, then gossip. Mr Trent had a great sense of humour and a lively imagination and the afternoons passed quickly as they vied with each other as to which of them could relate the best hospital story – one which, however preposterous, was just plausible enough to be believed.

Francis had always envied the ability of the upper classes to make light of practically everything – the more serious the situation, the greater the panache. He had never been able to decide whether this was due to incredible fortitude or simply lack of imagination – whichever it was, a stiff upper lip was obviously extremely useful in a crisis. So it was with Mr Trent, who was obviously in pain most of the time, but never complained. By mutual consent, they never discussed their illnesses, but confined themselves to the events of the previous day. Francis regaled Mr Trent with the saga of Mr Roberts while Mr Trent had scandalous tales to relate of the goings-on in the next room. Hawkeye was apparently looking for a bride – any bride – and nurses were offered jewelry and varying sums of money in return for their favours. Mr Trent had no way of knowing the outcome of these overtures, but the possibilities were endless.

Life in the main ward seemed tame by comparison, where, apart from the weather, conversation was invariably dominated by graphic descriptions of constipation – so much so that Francis often wondered if his fellow patients were capable of talking about anything else. Whereas, sitting in Mr Trent's comfortable armchair, there always seemed to be an infinite variety of subjects to discuss and, as the days went by, he looked forward more and more to their afternoon meetings.

"I say, old boy – guess what?"

Tea would obviously have to wait.

"Great fun and games last night – Hawkeye, at it again – gone too far this time though – been asked to leave at the end of the week."

Hawkeye had apparently followed Nurse Draper into the sluice in the early hours of the morning when everything was quiet, had pounced on her and carried her back to his room for a night of passion. Nurse Draper was a quiet little thing, she'd have been too terrified to struggle.

"Why didn't she scream?" asked Francis.

"Haven't a clue, old boy – didn't hear a thing myself."

The whole story sounded too good to be true, but the fact remained that Nurse Draper was mysteriously absent the next morning and Hawkeye was under a cloud. There was a conspiracy of silence among the nurses and they both concluded that Nurse Draper, her reputation ruined, had no alternative but to leave. They never saw her again, but the memory lingered on – the first nurse ever to be abducted from the sluice room. It was a good story and, when Hawkeye left, there was no one to contradict it. Encouraged by this success, Francis and Mr Trent redoubled their efforts to relate the most preposterous story until it soon became difficult for either of them to separate fact from fiction.

They also discussed religion and politics. Religion because, although both disliked churches and ritual, with their assumptions that Christianity was superior to other religions, it was an interesting subject – and politics because the fact that they disagreed so completely was in itself stimulating.

It seemed to them both quite natural that they could discuss their differences without rancour and Francis envied Mr Trent his confidence and self assurance. He always rose to the occasion and was seldom at a loss for words. The words may have been few and far between, but only because he chose to make them so.

Francis often wondered why Mr Trent was in hospital. He'd been on the point of asking him several times, but Mr Trent never talked about himself. He fought his own battles in his own way and that was obviously how he wanted it. The whisky bottle was never far away and, one afternoon, emboldened by a second dram, Francis broke their unspoken rule and asked Mr Trent what was wrong with him.

"Cancer, old boy – both lungs – won't be long now."

Francis sat motionless, drained of strength.

"Come on, old boy – drink up."

Francis searched desperately for something to say, something casual so as not to give way. He suddenly remembered that Mr Trent had said something about having been in the army for a while.

"Why did you leave the army?" he croaked.

"Too much killing, old boy – never did care for it."

Francis stood up and stumbled to the door.

"Going already, old boy? – not to worry – see you later."

Mr Trent's casual farewell was more than Francis could bear. He sat down in the corridor outside and tried not to cry. Mr Trent was dying, slowly and painfully, and there was nothing at all that he could do about it.

"Whatever's the matter?" Nurse Jarrett was kneeling beside him, full of concern.

"I'm, sorry, nurse. I feel such a fool."

"Don't worry about that. Come back to the ward and I'll make you a cup of tea"

She brought the tea and sat down beside him, waiting for him to say something.

"What's your name, nurse?"

She smiled. "Christine."

He knew it would be a nice name. "Well you see, Chris, I've just found out that Mr Trent is dying."

Her hand gripped his in sympathy.

"I know there's nothing you can do, Chris, but I just wanted to explain."

She sat beside him for a while and Francis lay on his bed, looking up at the ceiling. He kept seeing Mr Trent's thin face and he knew now why he had a private room, why they allowed him to have the whisky. The afternoon dragged on and he knew he'd have to carry on as usual. Tea time came and he walked slowly up the corridor towards Mr Trent's room, steeling himself for the encounter.

"Come in, old boy – sorry I upset you this morning – didn't think you'd take it so badly."

Francis made the tea and sat down. "What did you do after you left the army?" he asked.

"Went to Rhodesia – they call it Zimbabwe now, been there ever since – lots of friends there – knew I was ill, saw me off in style – damned good booze up – nearly missed the plane – told them I wouldn't be seeing them again because I was fed up with the sight of them – several crates of whisky to keep me company – they had to carry me up the steps to the plane – slept all the way to England – terrible hangover, of course."

He grinned at Francis and Francis grinned back. It was the longest speech he'd heard from Mr Trent, probably the longest he was ever to hear, but it was enough to remember him by.

He spent the evening prowling up and down the ward and biting his nails. He made his bed over and over again, pummelling the pillows. He tried to read – anything to pass the time – but the words blurred and he couldn't concentrate. Why did he have to knock on his wretched door in the first place? He need never have met him, then he would have died without Francis even knowing. People die every day, he thought, we all have to get used to it. Everyone we know is going to die, sooner or later. It was to be a sleepless night. How unfair it all was.

He heard the breakfast trolley, or thought he did, several times during the night. Why did all trolleys sound the same? At last, lights on, breakfast, and up the corridor to Mr Trent. He really must find out his first name.

"Hang on a minute – he's not ready yet."

Francis waited in the corridor and tried to stop biting his nails.

"You can go in now – no, don't worry about the tea."

Mr Trent was sweating profusely and his face was ashen. He opened his eyes and tried to say something, but his voice was so weak that Francis had to lean over him to catch what he was saying.

"Been watching television, old boy – Pope's Easter blessing last week – arm outstretched – reminded me of my Mexican cab driver."

His eyes closed and he seemed to be sleeping, then he opened his eyes and gave a half smile. "You see, old chap – Mexican cab driver always drives with one hand – other hand waving out of window – no matter how full – always room for one more."

Francis gripped the thin, bony hand.

"You see, old boy – maybe – just maybe – there's still room up there for one more."

He smiled again and his voice grew stronger.

"Sorry – not so good to-day – doped up to the eyeballs."

He handed Francis an envelope, addressed to some bank or other.

"Ask Sister to post this for me, there's a good chap."

Francis took the envelope from Mr Trent's thin, translucent fingers and he knew that Mr Trent was watching him, waiting for him to say something.

"Didn't know you did the pools," he said. "Perhaps you'll win first prize next week."

Mr Trent smiled for the last time and closed his eyes.

Time, thought Francis, for them to start moving over up there, making room for one more. Perhaps, if he was lucky, champagne all round to celebrate.

twenty-two

It took Francis several days to recover. It was bad enough having to put up with the tube in his back, squeaking away all night so that he couldn't sleep, without having to put up with all the idiots on the ward, moaning and groaning about their aches and pains.

"Excuse me."

Francis couldn't think who he was at first, then he recognised Mr Roberts, the little man they'd rescued from the broom cupboard.

"Where on earth have you been all this time?" he asked.

"In the bed – just opposite you."

Mr Roberts was obviously destined to spend his entire life being overlooked. He was so self-deprecating that Francis wondered how he'd managed to be born at all – let alone survive. He was clutching his hospital dressing gown with both hands and, small though he was, it only just met in the middle. He was probably worried that someone might see his pyjamas, or even worse.

"I wonder if you could tell me when the next service is? I've been listening to the morning service on the wireless, but there's nothing like the real thing, is there."

"I'm sorry," said Francis, absently.

He was trying to work out how Mr Roberts could have been in the bed opposite for a whole week without him noticing. Perhaps he was the perfect patient – never moving, never complaining, never waking up in the middle of the night, never refusing to eat his dinner, never asking for a bottle or a bedpan. How convenient it would be, he thought, to run a hospital where everyone did exactly as they were told, where everyone just lay there, never – ever – complaining.

"I. . . I'm sorry to trouble you."

Francis suddenly realised that Mr Roberts was still there, waiting for an answer – and, what was worse, he couldn't for the life of him remember what the question was.

"Glad to see you looking better," he said, playing for time.

"Yes, I am better, aren't I? Sister says I'll be able to go home soon."

He reminded Francis somehow of an Alice in Wonderland rabbit. He had large, pointed ears and his nose twitched constantly. People like Mr Roberts were doomed from the start, he thought. Kindness and gentleness were never enough, you had to be tough if you wanted to survive. It just wasn't true that the meek inherited the earth – they were trampled underfoot. He still couldn't remember what it was that Mr Roberts had wanted to know, so he tried again.

"How's the diabetes?" he asked.

"Oh, it's under control now, but Sister says I musn't drink any more Lucozade."

Incredible, fancy having to tell a middle aged diabetic not to drink Lucozade.

Mr Roberts backed away, smiling placatingly.

"I must go now," he said nervously. "Nearly time for tea. I hope they don't forget me again."

Francis suddenly remembered what it was that Mr Roberts had wanted to know – something about the morning service – but it was too late now and he didn't know the answer anyway. He watched as Mr Roberts climbed back into bed, still clutching his dressing gown with both hands.

A familiar ecclesiastical voice roused Francis from his stupor. "Sorry to hear about Mr Trent, but Sister tells me that he died peacefully, that there was nothing more they could do for him. But at least he died peacefully, secure in the knowledge that the Everlasting Arms were waiting to receive him."

What on earth was he talking about? Francis shook himself awake. He had a strong feeling that he'd missed most of the homily, which was just as well. He had a sudden inspiration.

"There's someone in the bed opposite who would like to see you. He wants to ask you about the morning service."

"I tried to have a word with him just now, but he seems to be asleep and I'd rather not wake him. I'll try again later."

Just my luck, thought Francis, he'd never get rid of the man now unless he attacked.

"Why do your people bless nuclear submarines?" he asked, aggressively.

"I'm not sure that they do."

Francis persevered. "Would you, yourself, bless a nuclear submarine?" he asked.

"We don't actually bless the submarines – we bless those who sail in them."

Francis decided to return to first principles. "Would you stick a bayonet into someone?" he asked.

"No, certainly not."

"Then why do you bless the Colours and preach about God being on our side?"

"I'm not sure that we do, these days."

No use, they were poles apart.

Francis closed his eyes and yawned. Perhaps the wretched man would take the hint and leave him in peace.

"Mr Roberts, can you hear me?"

Nurse Barker was leaning over Mr Roberts, her beautiful, pointed breasts almost touching his nose, but he seemed not to notice.

Some people have all the luck, thought Francis. Perhaps, if he closed his eyes, Nurse Barker would lean over him, too – so much more enticing than his previous visitor

"Sister, I think Mr Roberts is in a coma. There's an empty Lucozade bottle in his locker."

Francis was intrigued. Mr Roberts always did exactly as he was told and he knew perfectly well that he wasn't allowed to drink Lucozade. So why had he done just that? It was so completely out of character that the compulsion must have been very strong indeed. Perhaps he was hooked on Lucozade and couldn't face life without it. We all have compulsions, he thought – with some people it was sex, with others it was alcohol or drugs, gambling or making money – with Mr Roberts it was Lucozade.

"Search his locker nurse and make sure he hasn't any more bottles hidden away."

Sister gave Mr Roberts an injection and they waited for him to come round. "Diabetics do silly things sometimes. They'll go on for years without any trouble, then they go and do something stupid like this."

The insulin took effect almost immediately and Mr Roberts opened his eyes, blinking like an owl. Sister propped him up in bed and spoke to him, but he seemed quite dazed.

"Better leave him for a while. Keep an eye on him, mind – he's in a funny mood at the moment."

Francis still missed Mr Curry, with his good natured, earthy banter. The bed next to him was now occupied by a sad little man, whose wife was allowed to visit him at any time, so he must be quite ill. His wife was small and wizened and she darted in and out like a lizard, bringing him grapes and flowers. She never stayed for long unless she came with her sister, when they would stay and chat for hours, ignoring the object of their visit. They seemed to assume he was totally deaf and mentally deficient and he could doze off with impunity until it was time for them to leave, when he would wake up just in time for a parting kiss. Hospital visits, thought Francis, were rather like weddings and funerals – they provided a good opportunity for relatives to meet on neutral ground and catch up with the latest gossip.

"Anyone seen Mr Roberts?"

"He went to the bathroom, Sister. Just after the visitors arrived."

"You'd better go and check to make sure he's all right."

Nurse Barker returned almost immediately and went straight into Sister's office without knocking. The red emergency light went on and Francis heard Sister telling Nurse Barker to ring for Doctor Newman, before they both hurried down the corridor and he heard the sound of running water.

They brought Mr Roberts back on a trolley about half an hour later. He looked very pale and Doctor Newman came with him. "That was a close one, Sister, but I think he'll be all right now. Better put him in the empty side ward for the time being and get a nurse to stay with him until tomorrow in case he tries it again."

It was soon common knowledge that Mr Roberts had tried to cut his wrists, not very successfully, but seriously enough to cause concern. Francis wondered why he should have done it now. He was getting better and he was due to go home – so why now? He should have realised how Mr Roberts was feeling, how desperate he was to talk to someone. And he, Francis, had ignored him. Full of remorse, he asked Sister if he could go to visit Mr Roberts when he was better.

"I don't see why not, but wait until tomorrow – and don't stay too long. He's in Mr Trent's old room in the private wing."

Francis stood for a while outside Mr Trent's door, remembering the last time he'd stood there, the last time he'd seen him. It couldn't have been more than a few days ago, but he was already finding it difficult to remember what he looked like. He knocked on the door, half expecting to hear Mr Trent's familiar voice, almost resenting the fact that Mr Roberts was there instead of him. He could still hardly believe that he'd lost a good friend without even knowing his name.

Mr Roberts was sitting up in bed. He looked more like an Alice in Wonderland rabbit than ever, and Francis suddenly felt ashamed of himself. Mr Roberts was a real person too and he needed company just as much as Mr Trent – more in fact. Mr Trent had been sufficiently self contained, whereas Mr Roberts desperately needed to feel that he belonged somewhere, that someone cared.

"Mr Roberts, you have a visitor."

It was the little Irish nurse. How tired she looked, she must have been up all night. "Sister said I could leave him with you for a while. Don't go before I come back will you?"

"I'm sorry to cause all this trouble," said Mr Roberts, apologetically.

We're the ones who should apologise, thought Francis, for our indifference.

"What made you do it?" he asked, gently.

"I don't know really," said Mr Roberts. "Perhaps it's because I didn't want to go home – at least, that's what the doctor said."

Francis suddenly saw Mr Roberts at home, living his solitary life, getting up in the morning, making his bed, getting his breakfast, eating it in silence and washing up the dishes in silence, with no one to talk to until he went to work.

"What sort of work do you do?" he asked.

"I'm afraid I don't do any work. I often wish I did."

Francis tried to imagine what it would be like, doing nothing all day.

"What do you do all the time, then?" he asked.

"Well, I just potter around the house and do some cleaning, then I water the window boxes. And then. . ." He trailed off, miserably.

"Don't you ever see anyone?" asked Francis.

"Oh, yes – the milkman calls every day – and the postman, most days. My brother writes to me regularly – he's in Australia now – married, with two children. I miss him quite a lot, really, but someone had to stay at home to look after mother. She left me well provided for, mind you. She always said she would."

Francis understood only too well, a devilish pact if there ever was one. A life blighted and, in return, provided for. It usually happens to a daughter, he thought – it wasn't often that a son was trapped like that.

"Why don't you have a holiday?" he asked.

Mr Roberts gave a half smile. "Where?" he asked. "There's nowhere I really want to go."

"Nowhere at all?" Francis persevered. "Why don't you go on a cruise?" he asked. The very thought of going on a cruise made him shudder – sardines in a can, with nothing to do all day except eat, sleep and drink – but a lot of people went on cruises and thoroughly enjoyed themselves, so why not Mr Roberts?

"I wouldn't mind going on a cruise," said Mr Roberts, "but I don't want to go on my own. My brother and I planned a cruise once, but mother wasn't feeling very well, so we couldn't leave her."

Francis detected a faint note of resentment.

"Perhaps she didn't want you to go without her," he said, but Mr Roberts changed the subject.

"Do you believe in God?" he asked suddenly.

"Not really," said Francis, "at least, probably not in the same way as you do." But he was in for a surprise.

"I don't think I do, either," said Mr Roberts. "If there really is a god, why does he allow so much misery in the world?"

Francis was intrigued. Mr Roberts must be tougher than he looked. In fact, quite a hero, really, soldiering on, year after year – lonely, unhappy, yet refusing to invent a god he didn't believe in, just to make life easier for himself.

He decided to tell Mr Roberts about Mr Trent's farewell story – the story about the Pope's Easter blessing and the Mexican cab driver – and Mr Roberts listened intently, smiling to himself at the strangeness of it all. His whole face changed when he smiled and a certain confidence radiated, as if uncertain as to whether it belonged there or not.

"I've never been to Mexico," he said, "I've never even been in a taxi, but I think I'll go on that cruise as soon as I'm better."

They were still chuckling when the little Irish nurse returned. "Now what is it you're up to?" she asked.

"Have you heard the story about the Pope's Easter blessing and the Mexican cab driver?" asked Francis.

Mr Roberts looked away, trying not to laugh, but it was no use. He began to splutter uncontrollably. His thin arms flapped up and down and his high pitched voice squeaked with merriment.

"I really don't see anything funny in the Pope's Easter blessing," said Francis, trying desperately to keep a straight face. "I only asked if you'd heard the story."

Mr Roberts exploded again and the little Irish nurse frowned – someone was having her on, but she didn't know who, or why.

Francis decided to leave while the going was good.

"Mr Roberts will tell you all about it," he said. "As soon as he's finished laughing."

twenty-three

The room next to Mr Roberts – Hawkeye's old room – now had a card pinned to the door, a printed card with the name BERNSTEIN CONSTRUCTION. Someone had written 'Knock and Enter' on the bottom of the card, so Francis decided to do just that.

"Who the hell are you?"

A large, fat man with horn rimmed glasses was sitting on the bed, surrounded by books and files. Francis resisted the temptation to match rudeness with rudeness – a polite approach sometimes worked wonders.

"I'm sorry to trouble you," he said, "I didn't realise you were here."

"Who did you think was here – President Lincoln?"

An American obviously, and a rude one at that.

He had never really liked Americans and Mr Bernstein confirmed his worst prejudices – brash, aggressive and downright rude, he epitomised everything that Francis disliked.

"I'm sorry to trouble you," he said again, "I didn't realise you were so important."

The fat man didn't know how to take that. Francis knew he wouldn't. Thick as two planks, he thought, but cunning with it. He'd have to tread carefully.

"I'm Doctor Barker," Francis announced regally. "I've come to see how you are."

"Lousy, thanks – is that all you've come for?"

"Yes, that's all for the time being," said Francis, "except for the fact that those books and files of yours are probably full of germs. We'll have to take them away and disinfect them tomorrow."

"Is that so?" said Mr Bernstein, suspicious for the first time. "How come they let me bring them in then?"

"Serious oversight, I'm afraid," said Francis. "I'll have to speak to Matron about it."

He beat a hasty retreat. Enough was enough, it wouldn't do to be found out too soon.

That afternoon, on his way to visit Mr Roberts, Francis noticed that the small room next to Mr Bernstein's room had a similar BERNSTEIN CONSTRUCTION card pinned to the door. He couldn't resist a peek. It was full of office furniture and filing cabinets, with two telephones and a hatch which had been been cut in the wall between the two rooms. He peered through the hatch at Mr Bernstein, who seemed to be asleep, his black horn rimmed glasses perched precariously on the end of his nose. Then Nemesis arrived.

"Why are you annoying Mr Bernstein?"

No use pretending.

"Do you agree with private medicine, Staff?"

"I don't actually, but I don't see what that's got to do with my question."

"I only wanted to ask if you thought it was right for him to have two private wards all to himself when there's a shortage of hospital beds."

"Come off it. You know as well as I do that this room isn't really a ward – it's used as a broom cupboard most of the time – and it's none of your business, anyway."

"How about the telephones, Staff? Why should he have two telephones when the rest of us are lucky to have one between us?"

"Look, I'm a nurse, not an accountant. Why don't you ask him yourself? And don't forget, if there are any more complaints about your behaviour, we'll have to bar you from the private wing altogether."

Francis decided to ask Mr Bernstein about his two telephones – he could always combine it with some sort of apology. The notice on his door now said 'Knock and Wait' so he knocked and waited.

"Come," shouted an angry voice. "Oh, it's you – why don't you crawl back where you came from."

"I've come to apologise for annoying you," said Francis.

"Annoying me? – you can say that again. I haven't come here to be interrupted by idiots when I'm trying to work. Pity you haven't got anything better to do than bang on my door all the time. Why don't you mind your own business?"

Nothing like accepting an apology gracefully, thought Francis.

"I've also come to ask you if you think it's fair to have two private wards and two telephones while the rest of us have to share one telephone between us."

The horn rimmed glasses glinted.

"Has it ever occurred to you – asshole – that I have two private wards and two telephones because I'm prepared to pay for them. Maybe you should work a bit harder instead of loafing around all the time, then you'd be able to pay for what you get instead of scrounging off other people. That's what's wrong with this damned country of yours – you all want something for nothing and then you grumble when the money runs out."

Despite himself, Francis was impressed. The man was logical as well as articulate. He might be an out and out moron, but he hadn't got where he was for nothing. He suddenly felt a grudging admiration for Mr Bernstein, for his independence and fighting spirit. None of the old school tie nonsense for him. He'd fought his way up and he was jolly well going to make sure he stayed there. Pity he had to be so rude all the time, but there – what else could you expect from an American ?

"Fair enough," said Francis.

"What's fair about it? I never said it was fair – it's the way life is and it's time you grew up and stopped fooling around. Now get the hell out of here."

Suitably chastened, Francis went next door to visit Mr Roberts. He found him positively animated and the contrast between him and Mr Bernstein was so marked that Francis found himself resenting Mr Bernstein's bombast all over again. Why should people like him flourish while people like Mr Roberts had such a miserable life? Mr Roberts was busy with a pair of scissors, but there was no cause for alarm.

"I'm cutting out details of cruises, like you suggested. I'll send away for some brochures and find out what I can afford."

The change in him was quite remarkable. He was even teasing the little Irish nurse, inviting her to go with him.

"Why not? I'm sure you'd enjoy it. Separate cabins, of course."

"Mr Roberts, I'm surprised at you. Fancy saying things like that – I shall have to report you to Sister."

They were getting on so well together that Francis decided to leave them to it. Funny thing, fate. If Mr Roberts hadn't tried to cut his wrists he'd never have been given a room on his own and a nurse to look after him. He'd have been discharged from hospital without anyone knowing how he really felt. The world, he thought, was full of people like Mr Roberts, trying desperately to talk to people who hadn't time to listen because they weren't particularly interested. It was only by chance that he, Francis, and the little Irish nurse had been there to encourage him to laugh at things and to think positively about his future.

As he left, he heard one of Mr Bernstein's telephones ringing and his dislike of the man surfaced again. It *was* all so unfair.

Mr Bernstein, however, did not flourish. He had his operation a few days later and, by all accounts, it was a long and nasty one. The telephones were disconnected and the 'Knock and Wait' card was replaced by a notice which said 'Do not Disturb'. He gradually became weaker and his colleagues were sent for. They trailed in and out of the room in their smart, double breasted suits and stood around in the corridor, wondering what to do. They sorted through his letters and put them in files marked 'pending', but it was too late. Mr Bernstein was dead.

That night, overcome by remorse for having annoyed him, Francis dreamed that he was haunting the corridor outside Mr Bernstein's office, watching them take away all that remained – the office equipment, the files, the telephone and a huge telex machine, still spewing out useless information. The mourners picked up the sheets of paper and studied them carefully before putting them carefully in the appropriate files. Then they walked in procession down the corridor and out through the front door.

He lay awake afterwards, wondering where they'd gone. Perhaps Mr Bernstein would be knocking and waiting outside the Pearly Gates by now, cursing and swearing at being kept waiting, while his minions down below would be fighting one another for the succession. We don't really need a Hell, he thought, just a celestial view of what was happening down below would suffice. With any luck, they would keep him waiting long enough for him to take a good look at the disintegration of his earthly empire and he would writhe in celestial agony – that would be his Hell.

Francis felt less guilty now. He had, after all, no way of knowing how ill Mr Bernstein was and the confrontation between them had enabled Mr Bernstein to let off steam, so perhaps he had enjoyed his last few days, relishing what turned out to be his final condemnation of a way of life to which he was utterly opposed.

twenty-four

That afternoon, for the first time since his admission to hospital, Francis went for a walk in the garden. It was a lovely Spring afternoon, reminding him somehow of a weekend break in Berlin, three years ago. They had gone there to visit their youngest son Richard, who was on a school exchange. After trying to reach him on the phone, without success, they called at his hostel. He wasn't in, so they had gone sightseeing.

> Sitting outside a small café in the Ku'damm, soaking up the Autumn sun, listening to the hum of the city. Joanna with her big bright eyes, smiling at him.
> "Wouldn't it be fun," she said, "if he just came along."
> Francis resisted the impulse to remind her of the odds against meeting anyone by chance in a city of three million people. Joanna was undeterred, quite happy to wait for him, listening to the hum of the city, soaking up the Spring sunshine, feeling great to be on holiday.
> Unbelievably, there he was on the other side of the road, strolling along as if he owned the place.
> "There, told you so."
> Joanna shot across the road and pounced on him, laughing and crying, dragging him back to their table, hugging him in her excitement.
> "Great to see you, Pop."
> "You too, son."
> Onlookers smiling indulgently, happy because they were.
> No Wagner, no memorable sunsets, just an incredible feeling of well being.

The sun had gone in when he awoke and he opened the book of Kafka which he had borrowed from the library trolley, but it was heavy-going with all its doom and gloom. How on earth could it have found its way onto the trolley? Bequeathed perhaps by a disgruntled patient in the hope that it would make other patients miserable as well as himself.

He decided to have another look at it – it would help pass the time away, if nothing else. In the meantime, how about starting a travel agency? The possibilities were endless. It could be called Kafka Tours and, unlike most guided tours, they would contain numerous unexpected hazards, the most unexpected of which was the certainty that, the further you travelled, the less likely you were ever to arrive.

He lay awake that night, pondering the inevitability of fate. There might be more in this Kafka Tours business than met the eye. Let's assume, he thought, that they arrange everything for everyone, right from the start. It was difficult to imagine at first, but perhaps they arranged that as well, the difficult to imagine bit, so that people wouldn't know what was happening. They wouldn't realise that the whole world was controlled by Kafka Tours. They booked you in when you were born and booked you out again whenever it suited them. You kept thinking that you'd arrived somewhere, but you never had and you never would. Somewhere along the line you just vanished, like Mr Trent, and it was no use complaining – the Kafka computer had more important things to do than deal with trivial complaints about people vanishing.

Then why, he thought, why bother with us at all? We're excessively demanding and notoriously unreliable. We need organised religion to keep us happy and wars and space travel to make us feel important, so why bother? Why not concentrate instead on other life forms more amenable to discipline? It all seemed less convincing in the cold light of dawn, but Francis still found it preferable to religion. He read Joanna's lovely letter yet again and the black fantasies of the night dispersed. He closed his eyes and time stood still . . .

Roses are red my love, violets are blue, sugar is sweet my love, but not as sweet as you. Their first visit to Norway, a violin playing in a nearby cafe, the sound filtering through the open door as they sat outside in the sun, watching the little waves lapping the fjord, Joanna, relaxed, humming the tune as they waited for the little ferry with the blue and white funnel, just sitting there, feeling happy, content to wait, not really caring whether it came or not.

Twilight comes early in Norway, but it comes gradually, allowing time to plan the evening. They turned off the main road at a small sign which read 'Hotel Krone'. The sun was already setting, but the outline of a tall, gabled building was clearly visible, outlined against the yellow sky. They followed the road and soon arrived at a little town. The Hotel Krone was in the middle of the market square, still busy with traders packing up for the night. They parked the car and peered through the windows of the hotel. The dining room was already busy and they themselves were very hungry, more than ready for an evening meal and a room for the night. So they pushed open the front door and waited at the reception desk.

"Yes, of course, we have a comfortable room with a good view of the mountain and we will certainly reserve a table for you this evening. Allow me to take your case and I will show you to your room now."

They couldn't believe their luck. What a wonderful day it had been, and completely unplanned, too. They were really hungry and couldn't remember when they had last enjoyed a meal so much. They washed it down with a litre of strong red wine and decided then and there that this cheerful, bustling little hotel was the tops.

The centre of attraction was the Maestro. Tall and ageing, but still elegant, he played the piano so beautifully and with an air of such distinction that they decided that he could only be a retired professor of music, welcoming the opportunity of performing on such a splendid instrument. He paused from time to time to sip his wine and to acknowledge the applause with an old fashioned courtesy, his gestures more in keeping with a concert platform than a hotel restaurant.

Joanna was entranced and the Maestro, conscious of her pleasure, would smile and gesture towards their table with each encore. He had a thin, distinguished looking face and a little white beard, which made him look more Italian than Norwegian, and they wondered what had made him stray so far North – why he had left Italy, where the sun was less elusive and the hot, dry weather could have eased the arthritis which was already taking its toll.

They listened, enchanted, as the music of Strauss and Mozart wove its spell, his agile fingers skimming lightly over the keys, apparently unaware of their disability. Old Vienna lived again in the restaurant at that moment and, after he'd finished playing, they asked the waiter to take him another glass of wine, which he accepted graciously. Then, before leaving, they went up and shook him by the hand and thanked him for a wonderful evening.

They went outside for some fresh air before turning in and they were standing there in the crisp mountain air, when the front door opened and a tall, thin figure in a black overcoat walked slowly down the steps towards them. The Maestro paused for a moment when he saw them, then he smiled and raised his hat with a quiet dignity before turning and walking slowly up the street away from them. They watched as the dark, stooped figure disappeared slowly into the blackness, into the night.

That's all we ever do, thought Francis, disappear into the night. What was the point of creating anything if everything ended in nothing? The whole evening – the music, the happiness, the glimpse of immortality – what was it worth? And what did it all mean? The old man would be dead in a few years and he'd soon be forgotten, so what was the point of it all? Perhaps God – that miserable and sadistic old man – organised these moments of happiness from time to time as a diversion, a sort of bizarre experiment to assess the capacity of humans for self delusion. He must have known that they would need to invent Him in order to persuade themselves that their miserable lives had some sort of meaning. Then, in no time at all, the god they had invented would become their creator and they would bow down and worship him in the hope that, if they were lucky, He would allow them to live out their miserable lives and not die of cancer.

twenty-five

Francis awoke to find a large black crow at the foot of his bed.

"Good morning," said the crow, "I'm Father Preston. I gather that you're the man who disapproves of organised religion."

The crow was wearing a long black cassock and, to complete the disguise, its face was covered with a thick black beard, through which it spoke in a deep gruff voice.

"I've come to visit Mr Roberts," said the crow. "He's decided to enter the Church and I've agreed to accept him for training."

BLACK CROW STRIKES AGAIN –
STRUGGLING VICTIM HYPNOTISED.

"I thought he was going on a cruise," said Francis.

The crow flapped its wings and gave a disapproving croak.

"Mr Roberts wants to be ordained," it said. "We have decided that the cruise would merely be a distraction."

The crow fixed its piercing blue eyes on Francis. Perhaps it really was Father Preston after all. He must lose no time in warning Mr Roberts before it was too late – the man was more dangerous than any crow.

"Did you see Father Preston, Staff?"

"Father who?"

"Father Preston. He was here a moment ago, flapping his wings."

Staff looked at Francis, suspiciously. Another of his peculiar fantasies, she supposed.

He came to see Mr Roberts," said Francis, lamely. "He flapped his wings and he looked exactly like a large black crow."

"For what it's worth," said Staff, "Mr Roberts will be returning to the main ward to-day as soon as we've finished his blood tests, so you'll be able to tell him yourself that a crow has been waiting to see him."

Francis spent the morning reading Kafka until the dinner trolley arrived – cottage pie again, by the look of it. He was prodding at it uncertainly when he heard Doctor Warwick's quiet voice from behind the curtain which had been drawn around the next bed.

"I'm afraid it's no use, Sister."

Francis knew immediately that the man in the next bed was dead. Kafka Tours must have booked him out at this precise moment as soon as he was born. He was rather surprised to find that he didn't particularly mind – his neighbour's death made very little difference to him one way or the other. They were all in it together, he thought, fellow travellers on the same train, and the only ones you missed were the ones you knew. People alighted at various stops and just vanished, most of them so quickly that you never had a chance to say goodbye. The only thing you could do was to try to forget them and enjoy what was left of the journey, even though you never knew whether or not the next stop would be yours. The only certain thing was that you would never actually arrive at your destination. Kafka Tours would see to that.

His cottage pie congealed, uneaten, reminding him somehow of the corpse in the next bed. Francis suddenly felt sick – and guilty, because the corpse meant so little to him. He remembered his mother's corpse, all those years ago, small and shrivelled in its tiny coffin. That hadn't meant much at the time either, except for the shock of seeing her lying there, so small and vulnerable, but – apart from that – nothing, nothing at all. It was rather like that now. He felt completely empty, drained of feeling. His feeling of desolation grew and he knew that he couldn't just lie there any longer, feigning indifference. He had to get out of the ward quickly and breathe fresh air again. He did so long to be back home with Joanna and the children and the dogs, to hear the sound of the sea and smell the countryside and the green grass and be reminded that he was still alive. How awful it would be to die in hospital – alone, with curtains drawn around your bed.

He put on his dressing gown and stumbled towards the door. His eyes blurred and he knew that he was going the wrong way, that he'd missed the turning into the garden. The corridor was full of people in white coats, but he carried on straight ahead, bumping into them, heedless of where he was going.

"Steady on, mate!"

The broad northcountry accent brought Francis to his senses. He rubbed his eyes and stared at the man, stared at the bin he was pushing, full of waste materials, blood-stained swabs and bandages. It was 1942 all over again, but it couldn't be – that was thirty years ago – surely porters weren't still pushing filthy bin trolleys along hospital corridors? One didn't have to be particularly bright to realise the risk of infection. And yet, thirty years later, swabbing or no swabbing, hospital corridors were still dangerous places for patients and visitors.

The realisation that infection lurked on every corner had a salutary effect on Francis. What was needed, he thought, was a patients' union, to draw attention to all the things that were wrong. Even hospital consultants would be forced to recognise that patients were human beings instead of standing at the foot of your bed, just out of earshot, and mumbling among themselves as though you didn't exist.

The National Union of Hospital Patients would soon put a stop to that sort of behaviour. Any more mumbling, any more gratuitous insults, and the NUHP would call everyone out on strike. Patients who were still alive would discharge themselves and the Great Men would soon find themselves on the dole. The official pickets could always pretend to be dead if the going got rough – the police wouldn't dare touch them, just in case they were dead – nothing like a dead picket for stirring up public sympathy.

DYING PATIENTS COUGH DEFIANCE –
EMINENT SURGEON APPLIES FOR
NATIONAL ASSISTANCE. HOSPITAL
CONSULTANT DENIES MUMBLING

'Why did you mumble, Doctor Lloyd?'

'I wasn't really mumbling, your Honour. I was actually consulting my colleagues.' 'Call it what you like, Dr. Lloyd, we have heard ample evidence that you were mumbling. This is not only in breach of your contract, but is almost certainly the cause of the present dispute, which has led to seriously ill patients picketing the hospital instead of lying in bed. We can't have patients dying in the street, you know. The correct place for them to die is in hospital. The National Union of Hospital Patients has brought this case in the public interest and there is no doubt in my mind that your mumbling has been excessive. You will forfeit your private patients for a period of three years.'

The thought of hospital consultants having to forfeit their private patients cheered Francis up no end and he hurried back to the ward. He had to warn Mr Roberts about Father Crow before it was too late – but the enemy had beaten him to it. Mr Roberts was tucked up in bed and, hovering over him, was Father Crow's huge black cassock. Mr Roberts seemed mesmerised and Francis could hear his high, squeaky voice repeating some sort of prayer, over and over again.

He knew then that all was lost. He'd have to wait until Father Crow left before he could find out what had happened, although he didn't fancy his chances much now. Mr Roberts had needed a purpose in life and Father Crow had gained a convert. It was as simple as that.

Francis decided that the National Union of Hospital Patients needed a Charter. All unions needed a charter and the NUHP was no exception, so he roughed out a few basic principles.

One: Private Medicine to be Abolished.

Two: Private wards to be allocated according to need rather than ability to pay.

Three: No organised religion unless specifically requested. That should take care of Father Crow, he thought – and the parson, come to that.

Four: Physiotherapists to be prevented from inflicting unnecessary pain. Tricky one, that – they'd have to take professional advice before finalising.

He gulped down his tea. The important thing was a closed shop. Compulsory union membership for all patients was essential if they were to succeed. Perhaps this could be made a condition of their admission. The main problem, as he saw it, was one of continuity. Patients either died or they recovered and, as soon as they recovered, they were discharged. With such a high turnover, the NUHP was doomed before it started – unless they could arrange to have a few permanent patients as shop stewards. They could always earn their keep by delivering the post and the papers and by taking round the tea. This would give them plenty of opportunity to remind non-union patients of their obligations and, if all else failed, the tea could accidentally be spilled down the fronts of their pyjamas to encourage them to join.

"Don't forget, dear boy, as soon as you're better. . ."

Father Crow was on his feet, flapping his wings, ready for take-off. He looked exceedingly pleased with himself – the gift of instant conversion was not granted to everyone.

"Don't let that fellow get at you, now – and remember, the Lord's Will be done."

Mr Roberts smiled in a resigned sort of way and Francis knew he'd been outmanoeuvred. He never really stood a chance.

twenty-six

Francis couldn't sleep that night. The next bed was empty now, the mattress scrubbed clean in readiness for the next occupant, and it was as if the previous occupant had never been. Even his flowers had gone. Francis had begun to dread the nights when he couldn't sleep and everything was quiet. He would lie awake for hours, listening to his heart beating, listening to the poison in his lungs squeezing its way out through the tiny hole between his shoulder blades, squelching its way to freedom. The pressure would build up and the puss would gurgle forward with little squeaking noises, then it would stop for a while, then start again – a train trapped in a narrow tunnel.

Hundreds, thousands of passengers were waiting at the terminus – platform one for painless death; platform two for merciful oblivion; platform three for paradise and life everlasting; platform four for reincarnation. Kafka Tours had never lost a passenger, but they knew the importance of an apparent choice of destination. Passengers waiting on platform one heard the first train coming and a sudden dread descended on them. Perhaps, if they changed platforms, they could wait for the next train – anything to delay their departure, but it was already too late. The great black monster, curtains drawn, thundered into the terminus. Doors opened silently and wraith-like figures embarked in terror, then the doors closed as silently as they had opened and the monster, gathering speed, carried them away.

The next train was already waiting at platform four, where those expecting reincarnation were enjoying themselves, laughing and feasting before they boarded the train. Those waiting on platforms two and three – the huge central platform – became restive. They too were hungry and thirsty. It wasn't fair that the passengers on platform four should be enjoying themselves, while they went without. They crowded around the Kafka Tours representative, complaining loudly. But he pointed out that there was nothing to prevent them from changing platforms at any time, whereupon they drew back, fearful for their souls, content to have registered their disapproval.

A whistle blew and the merrymakers on platform four staggered to their seats, calling out to each other and slamming their doors and windows. They were still singing as the train gathered speed and thundered out of the station and into the long black tunnel ahead, leaving a dreadful silence in its wake. A thick, grey fog enveloped the central platform, preventing those waiting there from realising that the last two trains had already arrived, unannounced. The carriage doors opened and the passengers suddenly realised that their time had come. They had been waiting a lifetime, but they still scurried to and fro, uncertain even now which train to take. They could hardly be expected to know that the first two trains had already stopped in the tunnel, waiting for the latecomers. There was only one train and they were all in it together for their final journey – Destination Death. . .

"I wish you'd stop shouting – you'll wake the others."

"Sorry, nurse. I'm waiting for the next train. Have you ever been to Siberia?"

"What on earth are you talking about?"

"I was wondering if they'd double-tracked the trans-Siberian railway yet."

"Haven't a clue. I'm not a communist, you know."

"It's nothing to do with being a communist, nurse – lots of people go there on holiday. I just wondered if you knew."

"Well, I don't. It wouldn't suit me there – I prefer a bit of sun myself."

"How about all the people who go on it. How do they manage to come back if it's one way only?"

Perhaps he was going mad. He'd been having dreadful nightmares lately and he was finding it increasingly difficult to distinguish between fact and fantasy. He couldn't even decide if he was asleep or awake, half the time. Even now, speaking to Nurse Jarrett, he still couldn't shake off the strange feeling that they were on a train, in a tunnel – and there was no escape.

twenty-seven

"Good morning. I'm Doctor Nandi – I've come about your tablets."

Of all the wretched things, to be woken up in the middle of the night about his tablets. They never seemed to be able to decide how many tablets he needed. First it was two, then one, then three, then back to one again, as if his whole life depended on them – another of God's little jokes, he supposed.

"I'm afraid they're not here," he murmured, sleepily, "my locker's full of Lucozade."

Doctor Nandi didn't take much notice. He seemed preoccupied, as if on the verge of a momentous decision.

"I'm taking you off your tablets," he announced proudly. "Your tablets – you don't need them any more."

Francis was wide awake now and Doctor Nandi seemed to sense his concern.

"Don't worry," he said, "if God had intended your blood to be thinner he'd have made it that way."

Francis was staggered. What an astonishing thing for a doctor to say, when most of them spent their entire lives trying to rectify God's omissions. Doctor Nandi gave the ghost of a smile, almost as though he knew what Francis was thinking.

"Don't worry," he said again. "You can forget all about your tablets from now on – you're better off without them."

He switched off the light over the bed and was gone, as silently as he had arrived.

The tea trolley rattled, reassuringly. It had been a strange night, full of panic and foreboding. Francis could still see the railway terminus shrouded in fog, with huge black monsters thundering and hissing towards their final destination. Then there was Doctor Whatsisname...

"Nurse, what's the name of that Indian doctor who came to see me just now?"

"What Indian doctor? I really don't know what you're talking about. You've been talking to yourself most of the night."

He was really worried now. Doctor Whatsisname had seemed real enough, but perhaps that had been a dream, too. The only way to make sure was to wait and see if she gave him his tablet.

"Come on now, drink up."

"How about my tablet, nurse?"

"I'm not sure about that – you'd better wait until Sister comes. I'll ask her as soon as she arrives."

Chinless Wonder again.

"Turn over and let's have a look at your back. Hang on a sec'- there, that's got it." Francis felt something cold and slimy resting on his shoulder.

"I've taken his tube out, Sister – it was nearly out, anyway."

Francis felt cheated, somehow. He'd been waiting for weeks to get rid of the wretched thing. And now the great moment had come and gone and he hadn't even noticed. Sister came and prodded the wound, none too gently.

"Cheer up," she said, "you'll soon be going home."

Francis asked her about Doctor Whatsisname and the tablets, but she seemed not to know what he was talking about. She probably had more important things to do, other patients to see. Perhaps that's what's wrong, he thought – the word 'patient.' The poor unfortunate patients were supposed to be just that, eternally grateful for the crumbs of care tossed to them by generous doctors and nurses. Perhaps they'd be treated more sympathetically if they were called guests instead of patients, then there'd be no need for all that private patient nonsense and they could look forward to the day when hospitals were awarded five stars on the strength of their cuisine. The NUHP would certainly approve – all that was needed would be a notice in each ward – PATIENTS ARE OUR GUESTS AND WILL BE TREATED ACCORDINGLY. The thought of patients being treated as guests cheered him up no end. Why hadn't anyone thought of it before?

"I've just had an idea, Sister. . ." But she'd already gone and, in her place, stood a small black crow, peering at him, uncertainly.

"I. . . I'm sorry to disturb you, but I've come to say goodbye."

The voice seemed familiar and Francis smiled, reassuringly. It wasn't every day you met a talking crow, let alone a timid, talking crow.

"I'd like to thank you for all your help, but I can't stay long. Father Preston is coming to fetch me."

The crow's tiny wings flapped up and down and it was only then that Francis recognised Mr Roberts. He had on a black suit, a white shirt and a black tie, as if he were going to a funeral, and he was holding a small parcel.

"I. . . I do hope I haven't woken you up."

Mr Roberts blinked anxiously, apologetic to the last.

Francis had already forgotten what the little crow had just said, but it was something about thanking him for his help.

"I don't think I've been of much help, really," he said. "I can't even help myself much, let alone others."

"I wouldn't say that," said Mr Roberts. "You've helped me quite a bit and I thought you might like this – no, don't open it now – wait until after I've gone."

He looked round nervously and Francis saw Father Crow advancing towards them, his piercing, blue eyes gleaming with anticipation.

He stopped at the foot of the bed and glared at Francis.

"Come along," he said to Mr Roberts. "Time to go."

He spread his wings and enveloped Mr Roberts in the folds of his gown – and they were gone, as if they had never been. Father Crow had claimed his own.

"Did you see Father Crow, Staff? – Father Preston, I mean."

"Perhaps he's having coffee with Doctor Whatsisname."

No use, she didn't believe him. No one believed him these days. He suddenly remembered the parcel – that was real enough. He tore frantically at the wrapping. It was now or never.

"There, I told you about the crows, but you wouldn't listen – champagne. Real champagne, too – what a wonderful present."

At last, a suitable tribute to Mr Trent. What a shame he wasn't there to join them.

"Champagne all round," he shouted at the top of his voice.

"For goodness sake, be quiet. I don't know what's wrong with you – don't you ever think of other people?"

He untwisted the wire and pulled frantically at the cork until it shot out and hit the ceiling, triggering off all the despair and loneliness he had felt since Mr Trent's death.

"Here's to Mr Trent," he shouted, waving the bottle in the air.

All you ever got when you died in hospital was a paper shroud and a wad of cotton wool up your backside. Mr Trent deserved better than that.

"All right, Staff. I'll deal with this."

With remarkable agility, Sister snatched the bottle from his hand and poured herself a glass, then she poured another one and handed it to him.

"Here's to Mr Trent," she said, gently.

Francis drank, gratefully. He felt better now. A champagne cork instead of a twenty one gun salute – Mr Trent would have liked that.

"Don't worry," said Sister. "A lot of people get depressed after an operation and it isn't always easy to shake it off, but it's time you made a start – and you can start now by mopping up all the champagne you've wasted."

She was quite right, of course. He had wasted an awful lot of champagne.

Staff fetched a mop and Francis started to laugh. "You won't believe this," he said, "but I've done all this before, many years ago, though never with champagne."

The problem, he thought, was how to come to terms with a society where the weak went to the wall and the wicked flourished like a green bay tree, while the churches consorted with the establishment and paid lip service to those at the bottom of the pile. But it wasn't only that – his fantasy world had taken a bashing and that was much more difficult to come to terms with.

The world, he now knew, was no longer his oyster. Never again would he climb Mount Everest or make love to his favourite film star. Remote though these fantasies were, they had always remained possibilities until now. It was as though his heart surgery had hastened the approach of wisdom, so perhaps it was time for him to count his blessings and to accept gratefully what life still had in store.

Perhaps, if he calmed down, Kafka Tours would forget about him for a while and the inevitable would be postponed. The more he thought about it, the more he decided that Kafka Tours would have to wait – he still had a long way to go and he wasn't ready for them yet.